# Two Strangers

# and a Train

## Jennifer Jones

*For Chad Jones.*

"My heart is warm with the friends I make,
And better friends I'll not be knowing,
Yet there isn't a train I wouldn't take,
No matter where it's going."
~Edna St. Vincent Millay, *The Selected Poetry*

*Prologue*
*Upstate New York—2024*

April 20, 2024 materialized into a morning of reminiscing. I watched for what felt like ages as "angel's tears" watered the rose garden. Papa's words, not mine. I saw without seeing; instead, my mind's eye roamed back in time. When the sun peeked through the clouds, I imagined it to be smiling at me as its glow engulfed the large bay window in the common room. I, in turn, smiled back.

I wasn't supposed to lounge in the common room during these hours of the day. However, as I never caused any trouble, Betsy—one of the day-shift caretakers—turned a blind eye. Besides my claustrophobic excuse for a bed-chamber, this was the only quiet place within the confines of the nursing home —the only place that a lady could remember, uninterrupted.

Day by day, it became easier to give in to the conundrum of routine. *Take your pills, Ms. St. Clare, dinner is promptly at five, Ms. St. Clare, no, you may not go outdoors without a chaperone, Ms. St. Clare.* I wasn't allowed to think for myself any longer. Ahh, but my memories...those I refused to give away.

I stared, transfixed, as water droplets cascaded down the window glass. Padding behind me, Betsy sneaked cat-like into the room—presumably, to es-cort me to lunch. Even though my back faced her, wise to her game, I queried, "What day is it today, Betsy?"

"It's Wednesday, Ms. St. Clare," accompanied a sigh.

"Ah, pot roast followed by a rousing game of canasta, I take it?"

"Yes ma'am, you know it." Gripping the handles of my wheelchair, she gently pulled me back, then swished me in an arc as she cut across the common room floor. Another memory swayed along with the gesture. A lover once drew me across a ballroom floor—one much more lavish—as we waltzed in Vienna. That was another time...another life. It became my turn to sigh. What was it about rainy mornings and red roses that caused such notions to dance through my mind?

"Your hearing must be as sharp as a tack, Ms. St. Clare. Each day I try to surprise you, and each day you catch me before I do."

"You have a tell, dear heart."

A note of surprise registered in her voice. "Oh really? Now, just what would that be?"

"Your perfume. *Chanel No. 5*, I do believe?"

She giggled, "Of course. Yes, you're correct again."

"You have exquisite taste." Our conversation stopped short as we reached the dining hall. Raucous noise belied the commotion within. I cringed at the sound. Sensing my discomfort, Betsy walked around to face me.

She stooped and directed a warm smile my way. All the while, she feigned to straighten my sweater. Her scent, May rose and jasmine, enveloped me. It threatened to transport me back, yet again, to the past. She whispered, "Eat a few bites of the pot roast, and I'll sneak you an extra-large portion of chocolate pudding. Deal?"

I met her warm, amber gaze with a bright, cornflower blue one of my own. Along with my memories, it was the only other remnant of my youth. Betsy had to be about the same age that I was back then—when my life took the most extraordinary turn. I reached out to pat her shoulder and whispered, "You know, I was once young and lovely like you. My hair was much lighter, though."

"You're still lovely, Ms. St. Clare."

"Darling, we both know better."

She rolled her eyes as she changed the subject. "You know, I'm still waiting to hear another one of your stories."

The morning's indulgence flashed across my mind. "Well, I do have a story to tell you sometime—if you wish to hear it."

I get off work at three today. Maybe I can swing by your room then? We could catch a bit of fresh air in the rose garden."

"Of course, dear, that would be lovely."

Curiosity got the better of her. "Would you give me a hint? A good hint, now—something that I can daydream about during the rest of my shift?"

I drew her near—two conspirators, almost nose to nose. "I don't wish to give too much away, but I will say this: it's an enchanting story, dear, quite an adventure. You see, it's about two strangers...and a train."

*Paris—1936*

# Chapter One
## Cordelia

I jumped as the shrill call of the train's whistle pierced my ears. With gloved hands, I nervously smoothed my white traveling frock and sturdy, fawn coloured coat and made sure that my hat sat atop my sandy blonde curls just so. The worn, brown valise, which housed my meager possessions, rested at my feet, and my ticket, stamped 1936 April 20, peeked out of its front flap. Steamy mist permeated the cool morning air as I awaited boarding.

Days ago, I had accepted a governess position with the prominent LaRoque family. Newly stationed in Budapest, Colonel Arnaud LaRoque desired the accompaniment of his darling family. Lady Dahlia LaRoque had been eagerly searching for accompaniment of her own—someone to keep a watchful eye on her two young daughters. I fit the bill, as I was highly recommended by a close acquaintance who had utilized such services. Long story short, there I stood, poised on the platform, mentally preparing myself for the impending two-day-long trip and the life that awaited me at its culmination.

The train's sharp navy hue and luxurious golden accents mirrored themselves on the conductor's uniform. Though a frail, decrepit looking sort, his voice resonated along the full length of the platform as he bellowed, *"Tous à bord!"* The Colonel had sent for his ladies earlier in the week, which left me to journey alone.

Showcasing his wealth, Colonel LaRoque insisted that I would be housed in my very own sleeping compartment on the journey—without escort. It was highly improper for a lady of my station to be traveling in such a lavish manner, as well as without a chaperone. I was not surprised, though. I had already been warned, via the grapevine gossip, that the LaRoque household appeared rather liberal and unconventional in its running.

I sighed as I bent to retrieve my valise. I was anxious to remove myself from imagined whispers and prying stares and hole up in my compartment. I could freshen up there, as well as direct my meals to be delivered to avoid gossip. As I walked toward the conductor, with my ticket at the ready, I was sideswiped by a rushing figure. My valise fell from my outstretched hand. I yelped. I expected my rump to introduce itself, in a rather brusque *"how do you do,"* to the platform. Instead, a rough grip caught the front lapels of my coat. Leaned back, like a character in a romance novel, I stared deeply, and rather improperly, into the ebony eyes of my benefactor.

"Excuse me, Miss. I do apologize. Clearly, I wasn't paying enough attention," was spoken in clipped English.

I righted myself as I shot him a withering glare, "You should be more cautious." My face burned red hot.

"Yes, yes of course. Again, I deeply apologize." In his haste to catch my fall, he had also dropped his bag. I was surprised to note that it looked just like my own, as the man scurried to retrieve them both. He handed mine over with a chuckle. "Funny that our bags are practically identical."

Without amusement, I replied, "Oh yes. It's as if fate crossed our paths, just so we could be made the wiser."

He glanced around the platform, unheeding of my sarcasm. "Yes, well, if you've accepted my apology, I must be going. Don't want to miss the train, you know." He smiled. Underneath the boyishness of his grin, I could sense a touch of distress. I narrowed my eyes, curious, but let it—and him—be.

"Yes, fine, all is well. Run along and good day to you, sir." I was wary of this gentleman's antics, however my mother taught me to always display proper manners, regardless of the circumstance. Despite his restlessness, he replied in similar fashion.

"To you as well, Miss...?"

"St. Clare."

"Good day, Miss St. Clare. Safe travels." Again, his eyes darted about the platform with suspicion as he dashed toward the conductor. For what seemed like the hundredth time that morning, I smoothed my frock and adjusted my hat before I walked toward the train.

I handed the conductor my now crinkled ticket. He raised his eyebrow. Disapproval was written all over his face in dark, glaring ink. I assumed that he had witnessed the circus act that had just taken place. In defiance, I stared him down with cold, cornflower blue eyes. For some unknown reason he spoke to me in English, although his accent was thickly French, "Will Madame be needing any assistance with luggage this morning?"

I was fluent in both languages, however I spoke to him in kind, "No thank you, Monsieur. My luggage was sent ahead on a previous train, along with my employing family."

"Very well." He stared down his nose at my ticket, "Your compartment is located along the hallway to the right, then the third door on the left."

Walking down the opulent, yet narrow, hallway, I found my lodging just as he had stated. Locking myself inside, I dropped my valise to the floor, shrugged off my coat, and tossed my hat onto the narrow sofa. A washbasin, supplied with fresh, cool water, awaited my usage. I splashed a little water on my face and toweled off.

As the train rolled forward with a sluggish start, I slunk onto the sofa. It would shift into my bed come nightfall. Had I travelled with a companion, another bed would've pulled down from higher up on the wall above my head, in a bunk-like fashion. Thank heaven above, I was alone. The walls of the small compartment would begin to close in soon enough with just me here—especially during two days worth of travel.

I stared out the window for a time and admired the rushing countryside. Spring was my favourite season. Every year, I looked forward to Old Man Winter shrugging off his heavy, dull overcoat in favour of a lighter, green jacket. I hated to miss the final days of enchantment that April bestowed upon my fair city of Paris. Only yesterday, everywhere I turned, the heady blush of cherry blossoms transported me into a fairy-like realm. Now, the showy flowers were well out of my line of sight. For a moment, I closed my eyes and drank in the memory of the pink blooms like a fine wine, gently savouring every last drop of remembrance.

This was my very first trip by rail. I was amazed at the speed with which we bulleted through the outlying regions bordering Paris. I had only ridden in a motorcar once in my life. It travelled at eleven kilometers per hour, which at the time seemed quite swift. This train was traversing at approximately sixty-four kilometers per hour. It felt almost supersonic. The speed scared me at first, yet as I became accustomed to it, it served to lull me toward stupor. I did not wish to nap, though. Instead, I reflected upon my pending journey.

The train's next stop would be in Strasbourg, then another in Munich, and then on to Vienna, before trundling toward my final destination of Budapest. Some of the other passengers would continue on to Bucharest, Istanbul, or even Varna before the train looped around and wound inversely back toward

Paris. As I had never journeyed this far from home before, I was just a touch apprehensive.

It consoled me to recall that my father had also traveled abroad for the first time in April—April of 1918, that is—with His Majesty's RAF, or Royal Air Force, during WWI. On one of his meanderings, he spied a beautiful Parisienne—my mother—on the street. They both claimed it was love at first sight. After the war ended and my father completed his obligation to the King, they wed. He never returned to England. Paris became his home.

To support his new bride, he began working in my grandfather's *boulangerie*. Nine months later, *voila*, I arrived. As I grew, we were poor, yet happy. Mama and I danced while Papa sang and slapped his knees to make music. And we were always well fed, which was more than most could claim.

From the time I could walk, I also assisted at the *boulangerie*. I stood on a chair to hand the customers their purchases. They were all enchanted with this little honey-blonde, blue-eyed child, and looked upon me with as much fondness as my own parents. Ahh, those days. I believe that whether I am near or far, the smell of baking bread will always waft through my dreams.

After my *grand-père* passed, my father assumed the running of the shop. It was by no means a lucrative venture. As I came of age, I took on various side jobs to provide modest assistance. My recently acquired employment would provide the means to send a fair stipend home to my parents. Making them a little more comfortable would be the least that I could do to honor them. For, though they didn't pass along the riches of the world to me, they blessed my life with the only richness that counts—an abundance of love.

My disquiet was tinged with something else. Dare I say, excitement? No, that would be silly. I wasn't the type to become enkindled by such romantic notions. I couldn't afford to be that girl. I bent to access my bag. It didn't contain many items—a few necessities to complete my toilette, a couple of changes of undergarments, two more simple traveling frocks, and a well-loved, yet pristine looking, copy of Fitzgerald's *The Great Gatsby*. He and Daisy would serve to fill this compartment with romance, not I.

Unlatching my valise, my hands absentmindedly rifled through my possessions. They must've taken quite the profuse shake in my earlier accident, as nothing felt the way that I had carefully packed it the evening before. My hand struck something cold and metallic. Without thinking, I pulled the object out for closer inspection. "What could this possibly...?" I gasped as I stared down the barrel of a shiny black handgun.

How could this be? With trembling hands, I placed the gun on my now vacant seat. I scampered to double-check that the door was securely fastened and bolted. I did not want anyone to stumble into my compartment, only to spy what was, I assumed, a loaded gun on my sofa and begin to scream bloody murder. My heart raced.

After I assured myself I was locked in tight, I slumped to my knees and covered my face with my hands. I had to think. This couldn't be my bag! My bag must have gotten mixed up with the other gentleman's case in our earlier tussle. Had he noticed the switch by now, as well?

What was I to do? I couldn't very well announce to the staff that I had discovered a gun in my possession. I could picture it now—the arrogant conductor ignoring my insistence of ignorance, the cold steel of handcuffs tightening around my slender wrists, being thrown into lockup in a narrow hall closet until they could hand me over to the authorities. Panic, laced with details from the mystery novel I had finished the day before, pitched my daydream into a

8

frenzy. Perhaps reading that Christie woman's *Murder on the Orient Express* right before traveling wasn't the best decision, after all.                    I could return the gun to the bag—pretend it didn't even exist—hand the case over to the porter, and assert that it wasn't my own. But what would I say if they asked me any detailed questions, like had I searched the bag? I tended to become rather tongue tied when nervous, and I could not tell a lie with a straight face. My actions might rouse the porter's suspicions.

I had no clue who the gentleman from the scuffle was; he never divulged his name. But would they believe me? I held no confidence that someone in authority would trust a woman of my station. If they checked the bag, the whole affair would look rather unsavory. Could that bode poorly for me? What if they reported the incident to the LaRoques? I couldn't taint my character before my employment had even begun.

I needed to investigate more extensively into the bag. Perhaps I could locate some sort of identification. The gentleman boarded the same car as me; I could knock on every door, inquiring if there were a *"Mr. So and So"* within. This would be quite inappropriate, but if handled with enough rapidity, I wouldn't need to involve the railway staff. We could switch bags, and none would be the wiser.

As I delved inside, my fingers brushed against some sort of paper. I drew it out and found it to be a stack of pristine pound notes wrapped in a paper sleeve. There must have been at least fifty pounds in my hands. It was more money than I had ever seen in one sitting. Dread rumbled in the pit of my stomach, but I knew that I must continue searching. As the mouth of the bag dropped open even wider, for the second time that morning, I gasped at what I discovered.

# Chapter Two
## Victor

I stood sentinel in the doorway of my compartment. As difficult as it was to stand still, I leaned against the doorframe, a bored expression affixed to my face. Had anyone paid close enough attention, my roving eyes would have belied the calm demeanour my posture suggested. I lagged on a cigarette and searched the crowd for any hint of a dowdy, white frock or golden blonde waves.

Internally, I fumed. How dull-witted could I have been to allow myself to muddle my case with the St. Clare woman's? I had hoped to catch sight of her again. As of now, it appeared I would have no such luck. The growing noise of the conversing passengers in the hall grated upon my nerves and drove me inside of my compartment. I slammed the door. I'm sure this act garnered more attention than necessary, but vexation had taken over. Logic typically flew out the window first thing when I became stressed.

There was nothing that I could do about the incident now; there was no way to turn back the clock and stop the two bags from getting switched. Although changing the past was not an option, I could use my wits and the certain skill set I possessed to retrieve my bag. First things first, I needed to mentally organize the facts. My feet and my mind both paced within the confines of my compartment.

*Fact A:* Miss St. Clare appeared to be travelling alone. Accordingly, there would be no husband or chaperone to worry about. *Fact B:* It seemed that she was heading toward the same train as me. This meant that she was tucked away somewhere in one of these carriages. I could slip in and out anywhere on

10

this train with relative ease—just one of my many, afore-mentioned skills. That is, unless fate had other plans. But, no need to borrow trouble as of yet.

The contents of the bag, themselves, were against my favour. If she were to open the bag—which of course she would at some point—she might decide to raise an alarm. I hoped that this complication could be avoided. I had to move quickly. Every moment that I delayed brought me that much closer to the potential of getting caught.

I couldn't go through that again. I slumped onto the sofa. My head ached, and I rubbed my temples in an attempt to regain focus. As I knew that it would, my mind retreated back to the past. Try as I might through the years, I had failed to put it all behind me.

This trip down memory lane, as always, found me as a young lad still residing in London. I was practically a child then and had picked a pocket on a dare. It was a fool's errand. I learned the hard way that dares were rarely pulled off without consequences. I ran straight into the arms of the law, literally. Instead of this event scaring me straight and sending my life down a much different path, it turned out to be the first of many future run-ins with the Bobbies.

Shoving that particular memory back down deep, I got hold of myself. Yet, instead of focusing on the task at hand, my thoughts drifted to the St. Clare woman. Even though she was a bit too stodgy, she was certainly pleasing to the eye. I would go almost so far as to call her a work of art. Had I allowed myself, I could've drowned in the blue of her eyes.

I shook my head with disgust. I was behaving like a fool. I needed to get back into the game. With a renewed sense of purpose, I forced my rambling thoughts aside and made my way out of my compartment. I hadn't formulated a plan, but I was getting nowhere by hiding away. A gut feeling whispered that my path would present itself.

As always, my gut was accurate. A few moments later, I slipped into the uniform of one of the train's porters, which, as Providence would have it, fit me perfectly. I came across the unsuspecting sod as he navigated the now-empty hall just outside of my compartment. Upon spying him, a light bulb went off in my brain. I tailed him down the length of the train. After our "introduction," I leaned the poor bloke against the back wall of a linen cupboard, locked its door, and strolled back down the corridor.

After a brief stop in my compartment for Miss St. Clare's "lost luggage," I maneuvered toward the porter's office. I spoke to the porter on duty in decent French, although, being British, the words felt ridiculous and probably sounded even worse. As there were no others with the surname of St. Clare on board the train, I was given instructions to locate her within Carriage C, compartment 112. Hold the line—that was next door to my compartment!

I fumed once more. Because our bags had been switched, so had our tickets, thus, so had our compartments! How could panic have turned me into such an idiot? I remembered from my actual ticket, Jacques Marceau—the false name I had registered under—held down Carriage C, compartment 114. I had been holed up next door to her the entire time! I mumbled a hasty, *"Merci,"* then dashed away before I roused any suspicions.

Pausing outside of compartment 114, I breathed deeply. I scanned toward the left and then toward the right. This portion of the hall was still empty, but things could become extremely tricky were the St. Clare woman present within her compartment. I had to be most careful. I rapped on the door.

*"Bonjour.* Who is it?" Miss St. Clare's voice rustled like raw silk.

My heart sank. Re-establishing the French accent that I despised, I replied, *"Bonjour,* Miss St. Clare? This is, er…" I glanced down at the name badge affixed to the uniform I sported, "…*Monsieur Chevalier.* I'm one of the train's porters, and I've brought you your missing case."

Skepticism diffused through the closed door. "I haven't reported a missing case." My heart raced. I did not know what to expect from her. Locks were thrown back, then the door slowly opened. Suspicion emanated from her every pore. A flash of recognition sparked blue fire in her eyes as they met mine.

Without a word, she, too, glanced toward the left and then toward the right. Affirming that we were alone, she reached out, grabbed the scruff of my jacket, and pulled me into the compartment with such force that I landed face first onto the floor. She then locked the door behind her once more. "You!" she growled as she spun on her heel to face me, "You have some explaining to do! Or would you rather me call the authorities, first?"

On my back, in the midst of such tension, I still smiled. Damn, this woman had spunk!

# Chapter 3
## *Cordelia*

I scowled at the man on the floor of my compartment. "What will it be?"

"Relax, Miss St. Clare! I only tracked you down so as to retrieve my belongings."

"So that you could, what—use that?" I pointed at the gun still lying on my sofa. "And just how did you come across so many pounds? Or this?" I stalked toward the open valise and pulled forth a glittering necklace. Diamonds dripped from its gold filigree; the weight of them burdened my trembling hand.

"You don't understand..."

"You are correct, sir. And I do not wish to understand. Whatever you're involved in is most certainly no business of mine. I have a promising career waiting for me at the end of this journey, and I will not have that spoiled by the likes of you. Simply return to me what is mine and be off with your own wretched belongings. I will speak of this horrible affair to no one—on that you have my word."

"What job?'

"Excuse me?"

"Have out with it, then—your so-called 'promising career.' What is it?"

I sighed, my exasperation quite evident, yet my chest puffed with pride. "As if it is any of your concern, I am the newly hired governess to one of the finest families in Paris. We are relocating for the meantime to Budapest. *Monsieur* is well regarded within the ranks of the military and is required there. His capability and honesty have won him great favour." I shot him another withering glare, "Although, honest labour is something you obviously know very little about."

"A little presumptuous, don't you think, *ma chérie?* You don't know anything about my work ethic or me. You choose to stand there looking down your nose as you are carried toward your mundane life of 'honest labour.' But, never once have you known or will you ever know how dangerous and thrilling life can truly be!"

"Of all the nerve—Mr...?"

"Just call me Victor."

"Well then, Victor...I...you...gah!" I spluttered, then rolled my eyes and crossed my arms. He had sorely vexed me, this Victor. While he was correct in stating that I had never known any true thrill in life—other than from the books that I had devoured—he didn't need to know that he was so spot on. To avoid any further embarrassment, I changed the subject. "Are you going to spend the rest of the journey on the floor?"

"I wouldn't be on the floor at all, were your grip not so forceful. I think you may have broken a rib or two." He stuck out his lower lip, as if he were pouting, "I might die from the trauma—right here on your compartment floor! Then what would you do?"

"I'd leave you where you lie. Perhaps I would get a fair penny on the streets of Budapest for this fancy trinket of yours. Afterward, I could experience some of the thrills that you claim I know nothing about."

"*Touché!* Well done—that's the spirit, Miss St. Clare! *Brava!*"

"This is all some big joke to you, is it not? Nothing but a game."

He arose, dusted himself off, and chuckled, "Life is a most extraordinary game, Miss St. Clare." He laughed as I seethed. "You know, that necklace you're holding would look rather lovely encircling your neck. Even through that ghastly frock, I can tell that you have the bone structure for it. More's the pity that it must be passed along so quickly, or it would be worth a viewing."

I blushed as my hand automatically reached upward around my throat. This man was so disconcerting. I could scorch anyone else with my quick, sarcastic wit, but he seemed to feed off of it, which left me in a state of distress. "I, er, well—I don't know what to say..."

"It wasn't a marriage proposal, Miss St. Clare, merely an observation. Now, if you wouldn't mind, I would like to collect my things and head back to my own compartment."

"Yes, yes of course." I handed him the necklace, and as he reached out to retrieve it, our hands momentarily brushed. I gasped with surprise at the electricity of our touch. To conceal my emotion, I backed away and for the hundredth and first time that day, smoothed my frock.. What was that all about, anyway? I despised this wretched excuse for a man and the predicament that he had involved me in. Didn't I?

If he felt a similar spark, he did not reveal it. He placed the necklace and the gun back into his valise. "That seems to be everything. Just so you know, I didn't disturb any of your belongings. However, I am curious..."

"Curious?"

"In my line of work, I find that first impressions are almost always correct. Sticking to them has spared me from many a jam. That being said, you come across as a very no-nonsense, no frills type of woman. So why is one of your most cherished possessions a used copy of *Gatsby* of all things?"

16

"Ahhh, you think you know so much about me. Now, I am the curious one. Why do you think that it is one of my most cherished possessions?"

"Easy enough. You are obviously travelling light. I noticed this right away. Be aware of your surroundings, I always say. It was one of the things you chose to keep close to you. Perhaps it's just a loaner, but something tells me that isn't the case."

I looked away from his fathomless eyes. They threatened to unmask a portion of my soul. My voice softened, swept up in a wave of nostalgia. "It was a gift from my father. One day he came home with it tucked under his arm. We didn't have much money—still don't—and yet, he knows how much I love to read." Deep in my reverie, I smiled, "It was so shiny and new then. Up until that point, I had only read hand-me-downs or library editions. I had never seen anything so beautiful before in all of my life. And it was mine. All mine. I've pored over its pages so often that the newness has worn away. But, each time that I read it, it's like the story becomes new to me all over again."

I was overcome with homesickness. Looking anew into Victor's eyes, my own were met by a gaze, the meaning of which I didn't quite understand. I had never been looked upon in that manner before. It was a bit unsettling. I cleared my throat, defenses back in place, "Well, now—if that is everything, then you should probably leave. But, be cautious! I don't want anyone to see you sneaking out of my compartment. It wouldn't be at all proper."

The mysterious look on Victor's face vanished. "Don't worry," he winked, "I am always cautious." He dropped into a sweeping bow. "Miss St. Clare, further apologies for entangling you in yet another mess. I will attempt to avoid involving you in anything more before my departure tomorrow."

"Oh, will you be taking leave in Vienna? Or Budapest?" A sly grin crept across his face, which caused my cheeks to flame. "N…not that it matters, mind you. Just thinking aloud," I stuttered. I felt the flush extend down my neck, molten in its intensity, "I'm…I'm merely curious, of course."

"Of course." His sarcastic tone lightened as he proceeded. "Vienna is the plan. You will be keeping that little detail to yourself, I assume."

"Yes…but…" My brow furrowed.

"But what?"

"I am surprised you would divulge such information to me. I honestly didn't expect you to answer." I prattled on, "Why would a man in your line of work trust someone such as me with your sensitive details? Do you plan on murdering me?" Unease engulfed me at the thought.

"What the devil are you talking about?"

I spluttered, "I thought that gangsters offed anyone who knew too much."

He cackled. "I am far from a gangster, Miss Saint Clare. I've never, as you say, 'offed' anyone. I think that someone has been reading too many detective novels in her spare time."

I gained a bit of composure. My cheeks burned, "Even so, you evaded my original question."

"Perhaps I think you have a trustworthy face."

I wasn't sure if his answer was permeated with arrogance, ignorance, or false flattery. "At any rate, my lips truly are sealed."

"Good girl. *Au revoir*, Miss St. Clare."

Without another word or glance, he sauntered toward the door. He opened it and craned his neck both toward the left and then toward the right, as I had done, not ten minutes previously. Satisfied, he slipped into the corridor and shut the door. I rushed forward to peer into the hallway and follow his progress, but it was empty by the time I reached the doorway. As quickly as he had entered it, Victor had strolled right back out of my life. Or so I thought.

*Strasbourg—1936*

# Chapter 4
## Victor

A joyful, bordering on the insane, grin stretched across my face. I was so close to making my way out of this bloody country! After my quick departure from Miss St. Clare, I whiled away the remainder of the first leg of the journey by napping in my compartment—with one eye open, of course. As the train hastened ever closer to Strasbourg, a member of the staff came round to report an impending three-hour layover—longer than average—due to some malfunction. I was assured that it was no more than a glitch. He encouraged me to take advantage of the delay by exploring the enchanting city. After his departure, I groaned. I had spoken too quickly.

Passengers were cautioned upon departure to return to the station by no later than 6:30 pm. The train would need to dash toward Munich after such a lengthy stopover. Failure to observe this guideline would mean being left behind. I did not wish to spend one second more than necessary in this country, so my intention was to comply in full.

Fingers crossed, nothing unexpected would befall me during my explorations. I seemed to be finding myself in more and more sticky situations, as of late. I wondered if I should quit the game for good? Perhaps I was becoming too soft...too distracted. At any rate, I needed to fly under the radar between here and Vienna, especially after what had just taken place upon the train. I trudged along, one with the masses, toward the open side door. As much as I disliked to admit it, a few hours of freedom did sound rather appealing.

Railway staff tended to a random man a bit further up the hallway. He held an ice pack to his left temple, and his right eye appeared to be swollen and bruised. It was the porter I had walloped earlier! I pulled my hat down a little more snugly about my brows and held tightly to my bag. Could this bloody crowd move any faster? Ahh, freedom—mine, at last!

The city's quaint streets held my attention. Although I wasn't enthralled with wasting more of my time in yet another French city, meandering topped being reported to the law—by a longshot. I also prided myself on being a rather positive-thinking sort of chap. One should make the most of the time given to him. I passed the spired, Gothic cathedral in the city centre—it was a sight to behold—and listened in as a tour guide instructed her group about the astronomical clock that brought said cathedral its fame. Although my French was far from extensive, and the tour guide's English was rather broken, I followed the basic gist with genuine interest.

All seemed to be well, until I passed through the Place Kléber. The buildings were breathtaking, yet somehow I couldn't tear my eyes away from a cart at the edge of the square. It boasted some rather delightful looking tarts and pastries. I was as tempted to sample the delicacies as I was the dark haired beauty selling them. I sauntered over. She giggled receptively at my flirtations, and I readied myself to make a move.

I glanced over her very kissable shoulder to take stock of my surroundings—old habits never die. I noticed a man lurking in the alleyway adjacent to a nearby building. He stood in shadow and his Borsalino hat angled just enough to conceal his identity. He appeared to be watching me. He moved out of the shadows and slightly bowed as he removed the hat. Panic rumbled in the pit of my stomach as sunlight glinted off the tin that covered half of his face. I recognised him instantly.

Sometimes, during life's journey, one might make a mistake when passing someone on the street. Perhaps one would do a double take or even go so far as to call out a name before recognising that the particular person was not the anticipated one. But, with some people, there was simply no question. Perhaps it was the menacing way that he stood, or perhaps it was the half a sardonic grin that he wore—whichever did not matter. My veins turned to ice.

The mask, a medical invention designed to resemble a human face, was worn by soldiers who had become disfigured due to combat. Rumour stood that this particular gent donned his after having been gassed in the War. Rumour further suggested he was the number one cronie for a certain, high-ranking member of Marseille's Carbone-Spirito clan. To me, he was simply known as Forte. How benign the name sounded, but the simplicity of the moniker belied the nature of the man who assumed it. He was cunning, ruthless, and he did not care who he trampled upon—as long as he came away with the largest share of the spoils.

Technically, the necklace, as well as half of the £50 in my pack, belonged to him. He appeared to have come to collect. Judging from the cold look on his face, it was obvious that he knew that I had attempted to steal away with it all. It had been idiotic of me to think I could run from the likes of him. He patted his trouser pocket and grinned. The motion indicated that I wasn't the only one carrying a weapon.

When faced with a situation such as this, one has two choices: stand and face the proverbial music, or run as if the devil were at your very heels. Being a true thief—and even truer coward—I chose the latter. I bolted without so much as a goodbye peck for the pastry girl.

How many corners I turned, I did not know. The buildings all blurred into carbon copies of one another as I ran. All I did know was that I still had a half an hour until the train departed. I couldn't return to the station. He would easily figure out my destination, were he to intercept me there, if he weren't wise to that fact, already. Instead, I made my way back as close as I dared, then darted into a fairly busy *café* a few streets away from the train. I dropped into the first empty chair that I found. A familiar voice greeted me.

"Victor? Are you stalking me now?"

It was the St. Clare woman! I gazed upon her in disbelief. I couldn't wrap my brain around whether she was being serious or not about the stalking. I was still in a bit of a panic from my encounter with Forte. I groaned. Out of all of the people on the train, or even in Strasbourg, how could she be sitting across from me?

"Who are you hiding from?" she whispered, leaning in.

"Miss St. Clare! What in blazes are you doing here?" I cried in response.

In a haughty voice, she replied, "I couldn't very well stay on the train, could I? I needed some fresh air, you know, a change of scenery. This seemed like a reasonable spot, but I wasn't prepared for the gentleman in the corner." A superior look crossed her face. "He smells rather strongly of rum and seems to have vomit on his sleeve." She wrinkled her nose in disgust.

The lady had a point, as the man did appear to be quite inebriated.

"Shall I repeat my question?" She crossed her arms and cooly assessed me.

"What makes you think that I'm hiding?" I replied with a little too much force.

"Isn't it obvious?" She leaned back, her eyebrow arched, "You are behaving even more evasively than you were in Paris or on the train, your eyes won't stop darting toward the door, you're sitting in an artsy coffee shop—which I do not believe to be your sort of establishment—and your knuckles are so white from gripping onto your bag, that they seem they might pop off at any moment. Need I say more?"

Damn this woman! I looked down and realised she was correct, then checked the door, once more, for good measure. Had I become this transparent? "Look," I started, "you truly don't want to know." I attempted to play it cool, "It's a long, boring story, nothing like *Gatsby*. You wouldn't want to hear it."

She sized me up as I pulled my hat down over my brows and slid my bag under the table. Awkward silence held the two of us captive. "I'm sure that your, and I quote, 'boring story' wouldn't rival my *Gatsby*. Still yet, you've piqued my interest with your behaviour." It surprised me when she arose, " Even so, I should be going. I do not want to miss the train." She pulled her own bag from under the table. "Goodbye, Victor. Although, with the way events have transpired thus far, I wonder that our paths will not somehow cross again".

I began to sweat. What if Forte waited for me outside of the coffee shop? I had no idea what to do, if that were the case. I only had to conceal myself long enough to make it back to the train. I needed a plan. Just then, realisation stomped upon my toes.

"Miss St. Clare, please wait." I attempted a calm demeanor as I also stood. I shook inside, but I smiled and spoke with poise, "I'd like to escort you back to the station, if you would permit me to do so."

The look of surprise that registered across her face was slightly amusing, even though I wasn't in the state of mind to laugh. Her shock quickly changed to laughter. She chuckled all the way to the door. I slumped back into my seat and laid my head down on the table; I had only one hope left.

Her voice rang out next to me and caused me to jump. "Well, don't just sit there napping—come on then." I couldn't believe that she stood beside me, once more. "Remember, we've got a train to catch." I nodded—steady now, old chap—pulled the bag from under the table, and followed her to the door. Okay, I thought to myself, make that two hopes.

~*~

The train station arose within view; I thought that perhaps we were in the clear. As if from out of nowhere, though, Forte materialized. Again, he leaned in the shadows, and again, the view of his face twisted my stomach into knots. I wasn't certain that he had seen us. Hope surfaced once more. Miss St. Clare walked to my left, and I attempted to crouch beside her, out of view. She didn't notice my antics. From the time that we left the café, we hadn't spoken much, but it wasn't an uncomfortable sort of silence. We continued on, as such. She was unaware that we were being followed, and if I played my cards right, it could remain that way.

We had made quite a bit of headway, and once again I thought that we were free of the dreaded man. Hope dashed itself to bits as he fell in line behind us. He strode at an alarming pace. I had to act. "Miss St. Clare..." I uttered.

"Yes?"

Survival kicked in, full force. I grabbed her and pulled her in between Forte's swift approach and me. After that, I don't know what happened. Perhaps the colour of her eyes caught me in their grasp or perhaps it was the thrill of the moment. Whichever, even though the devil rushed toward us, I couldn't help myself. I passionately kissed her.

Had this been a romance novel, the universe would have smiled upon us and provided an improbable means of escape. We would have fallen madly in love and dashed away into a rose gold sunset. The End. Alas, none of these even came close to occurring. After her initial shock, she both pulled back and shoved me away in the same motion.

"Have you gone mad?"

"Run!" I shouted in response.

She had little choice, as I grabbed her elbow and sprinted forward. She stumbled; I thought she would fall. Forte was right behind us. My little romantic gesture had cost us a major amount of time. In an attempt to distract him, I threw the bag that I carried as far down an alleyway as my strength would allow. Miss St. Clare righted herself, so I locked a talon-like grip upon her hand and continued running.

We dashed into another nearby alley, out the other end, and rounded a corner. Pressing our bodies flat against the doorway of the closest storefront, we hardly dared to breathe. We waited, and waited, and waited some more—but he was nowhere to be seen. Perhaps my little trick had worked, after all.

We wandered to the end of the street. My nerves stretched taut, like a violin whose strings were in desperate need of tuning. Up until this point, Miss St. Clare had remained as still as the grave. Now that the danger didn't appear to be quite so imminent, she refused to hold back any longer. "I have never..." she spluttered, "EVER...been so disgusted..."

"Miss St. Clare... "

"Insulted..."

"Miss St. Clare..."

"EMBARRASSED!"

I shouted, "Miss St. Clare—for the benefit of myself, France, and the northern hemisphere at large—please SHUT UP!"
She sucked in a breath, her face splotched with crimson, then spluttered like a wet hen, unable to respond. She halted in her tracks, and proceeded to burst into tears.

A few dramatic crocodile tears were the least of my worries, but she simply wouldn't budge. I couldn't just leave her there. What was I to do now? "Miss St. Clare..." my voice softened.

"Don't!" Her tears welled on. She pulled her bag open, and the weeping ceased. In an instant, her face morphed into seething rage. As she yanked the necklace from out of my bag, not a handkerchief from out of her own, the hope I had counted on in the *café* had come to light. I had swapped them, once again. The bag that I had tossed into the alleyway to divert Forte had, in fact, been hers.

She slapped my face, as only a scorned woman could. Wow, that smarted! There was no time for tears of my own, though. Nursing my inflamed cheek, I thrust my pocket watch toward her as I ventured to both diffuse the situation and revisit our surroundings. "Check the time. I think that we really should get back to the train." Her expression changed from red hot to stark and pale in an instant. "What? What's wrong?"

Her eyes were wide, "The, the train..."

"Yes, the train...what about the bloody train?"

Her voice sank, defeated, "The train was due to leave five minutes ago."

# Chapter 5
## Cordelia

My heart sank. I was now stranded in an unfamiliar city with an unfamiliar man. All the while, the train chugged onward toward its destination—my destination—only, without my presence. In all of my life, I had never been consumed by such dejection. I slunk to the front stoop of the corner storefront and languished in my despair.

Victor waited nearby, shuffling his feet. It was obvious that he recognized my duress. "Miss St. Clare, I know that this seems like quite the setback, and I promise you, we will figure it all out. But, we really must go. That man…"

Hell's fire blazed white-hot in my blue eyes, as I leapt to my feet. "My name is Cordelia…CORDELIA, do you hear me? Furthermore, do you have any idea of what you've done? Do you? You crack wise about my lack of experience, and spout off your flippancy—*'Life is a most extraordinary game, Miss St. Clare.'* And yet, you obviously know nothing at all about life. Not real life. Life is about duty, responsibility—serving a purpose. But not yours—oh NO! You dash around, a man about the world, with your trinkets and your money and your guns—but without a clue as to how life really works."

My throat was sore from shouting, however I hardly noticed. I prepared to continue—with all of today's stress, it felt good to let go—but I stopped short as a sneer curled Victor's upper lip. His voice emanated the powerful sort of quiet that one feels as well as hears, like just before a massive thunderstorm.

"I'm the clueless one, you say? I'm the clueless one? You walk around with your airs and your graces and your books and your stories—*'Oh, we were poor, but my Papa was so kind…'* blah, blah, blah." His tone shifted to a jeer, "Do you want to hear a story, Cor-deelia, hmmm? I've got a good one—could be a bestseller. It's about a boy who never even knew his *Papa*, or his mother, for that matter. A boy who was left as a toddler on a doorstep in a back alley in the Limehouse district. Abandoned. That boy didn't even have the luxury of being shipped off to the workhouses or a bloody orphanage. His home was the street. His reality was that if you wanted it, you had to steal it. He stole to survive. And yet, according to the likes of you, he's the clueless one." The warmth in Victor's eyes had been replaced with cold bitterness. And pain.

My rage dissipated as quickly as it had come on. It was replaced with embarrassment and a bit of guilt. I sucked in a breath, "Oh, Victor—I..."

"I don't want your pity," he growled. "However, I do want you to calm down. Even though you think otherwise, I happen to know a thing or two about honour. Somehow, some way I will get you back on that train. It's the least that I can do for getting you involved in my mess." His gaze dropped and he took a deep breath. His tone softened around the edges, "It seems like we've given Forte the slip for now. Let's head back toward the station and weigh our options."

We began to walk in the direction from which we had originally come. I wrapped my arms around myself, not from chill, but from misery. The silence between us hung heavy, both with words unspoken and words unable to be re-tracted. I finally dared murmur,"Forte? That's the name of the man who was following us?"

"Indeed."

"Who is he? And what does he want with you?"

"Quite the curious little kitten, aren't we?" Victor dryly chuckled. It seemed we were on speaking terms once more. Our previous argument had been, at least temporarily, laid to rest. "He's an old acquaintance of mine—a business partner, if you will. What he wants from me is that trinket in my case and, I'm sure, all of the cash in my possession. Though, to be fair, only half belongs to him."

"You stole from him?" I was incredulous.

"Stop acting so surprised. I'm a thief. It's what I do." He shrugged, "And, besides, don't you think that he would've done the very same to me, if given the opportunity? Of course he would've. I just beat him to the punch."

"And now he's come to collect what he's due?"

"I'm afraid so. I didn't think that he could have caught up to me so quickly, though, me jumping the train and all. Bloody bugger. I thought that my plan was rather foolproof: make my getaway, hop the train, meet up with another business partner in Vienna, hock the trinket, then drop off the face of the earth with all of the cash. The End."

"Fancy plan." I rolled my eyes.

"I thought so, too..." he paused. "Wait a minute. Was that sarcasm that I just detected, Cordy?"

"How ever did you guess?" I sighed, "Victor—did you seriously think that your so-called plan would succeed? Have you never read a detective novel before?" I stopped short, "Cordy, you say?" Again, I rolled my eyes. "I don't think so—not in a million years."

He grinned, "Not all of us have the time to be whiling away the hours reading and the like, Cor-deelia. There, is that better?"

Typically, I would've found someone like him to be rather irksome. Even though I knew that I should be enraged, or at the least, quite annoyed with him—somehow, I wasn't. We merged into a tour grouped by the statue of

32

the Place Kléber's namesake. In normal circumstances, I would've been interested to hear the guide explain that after Jean Baptiste Kléber's assassination in Cairo, his remains were buried in a vault and laid to rest underneath the statue we now viewed. But my insides shook, so the facts flowed over me without sinking in.

Victor scanned the horizon for the whereabouts of Forte. As much as we wished otherwise, we knew in our hearts that he would make another appearance. We skirted the crowd and prepared to dart toward the train station, when a scream resounded, closely followed by a gunshot. Pandemonium ensued, as terrified bodies dashed to and fro. Pivoting momentarily in the direction of the shot, Victor yelled, "He's over there! He found us!" Victor latched onto my arm with a talon-like grasp and jerked me toward the nearest street.

Forte had become ensnared in the crowd's mass exodus, which bought us just a few precious moments of time. No cover could be found within the square; we didn't know in which direction to turn. Victor attempted to retrieve his own gun from his bag, but in his fear, he fumbled with the latch. The devil had almost freed himself from the crowd. Soon, he would once again aim his weapon at us. This time, I felt certain that he wouldn't miss his mark.

I was beyond terrified. Just as hope had almost completely deserted me, an extraordinary sight materialized. A stunning, black car screeched to a halt on the path before us. It gleamed so brightly that it appeared to be made of ebony glass. I had never laid eyes upon something so luxurious. Given the peril which surrounded us, I wondered if it were even real. Perhaps I had finally gone mad.

The stranger behind the wheel shouted, "Hurry, young people. Get in. Now." Our minds and bodies being of one accord, Victor and I raced to the awaiting motorcar and piled into its sumptuous back seat without a moment's hesitation.

With a squeal of rubber, the motorcar shot forward. I watched with horror out the back window as Forte stood in the street and aimed his gun toward our quickly retreating vehicle. He appeared to let out a wail of frustration as we deftly motored out of harm's way. Our mysterious benefactor spoke, "It's a good thing that bloody madman didn't graze my car with one of his bullets. There's only one other like it in existence, don't you know?"

Being the consummate man, Victor talked shop with the stranger, "It's quite the tin can, Mr...?"

"Actually, it's Air Commodore Charles Frederick Algernon Portal. But my friends call me Peter. And, you like her, do you? She's quite lovely, isn't she? She's a 1936 Voisin C28 Clariere. Just listen to her purr. That's a 3.3-liter motor under the hood. Magnificent...simply magnificent. And, smell that leather, would you? She sports aircraft design, I tell you...aircraft design. Of course, I am an airman, so it makes perfect sense. Did I mention there's only one more like her in existence?"

"I believe you did, Commodore..."

He blazed forward, across the *Rue de Francs-Bourgeois*, continuing with his tale. "That one was delivered earlier in the year to the French embassy in Berlin—placed in the care of a Mr. Le Feule, I do believe. Well, I said to myself, we can't have the French be the sole possessors of something of this calibre, can we, my boy?" He chortled, full of mirth.

His dark eyes radiated mischief in the rear view mirror. He seemed decent enough. I analysed as much of him as I could scan from my meager vantage point. Thinning, dark hair, combined with elfin ears, and a profile's view of a full nose and lips did not offer many clues into his heart or the motivations within it. Victor's tension and suspicion seemed to have tarried far behind with Forte. Some criminal he was! He leaned forward, eyeing all of the details of the car's interior while the two men, or should I say boys, carried on with their conversation.

"Excuse me, please, sir..."

"Why, apologies, dear lady! I had quite forgotten you were with us— quiet as a mouse, you are! This talk has to be boring beyond belief, my dear. And do call me Commodore."

"Right, um, Commodore," I spoke with earnest, "where are you taking us, please?" A neighbourhood of black and white timbered buildings blurred within the frame of the window as we raced madcap along the narrow streets that surrounded them. I became hopelessly lost as they whirred past.

"Why, away from the madness, lovely lady. What is this world coming to? I thought we had all learned our lesson after The War regarding maniacs toting weaponry!" He shook his head with disgust.

I took a deep breath, "That's wonderful—all well and good—and thank you. But, now that it seems that the turmoil is behind us, what exactly are your intentions?"

"Ohhh, right—I hadn't quite gotten that far. Got caught up in the excitement, I did." He chuckled, "I can drop you wherever you wish, young people. I think we've sufficiently made our way out of the danger zone."

"We aren't from Strasbourg," Victor interjected, "we missed our train. I made a promise to Cordy here to get her to Munich, so that she could catch up and re-board. She's heading to Budapest."

I vehemently whispered, "Victor—why don't you go ahead and tell him my birthday and my bra size, while you're at it? We don't know this man." He gave a lopsided grin, "*Ooh la la*, Cordelia. When I figure those out, *ma chérie*, I'll be certain to share."

I crossed my arms in disgust, and turned toward the window. The Commodore didn't miss a beat, "Munich, you say? Good luck with that, young people. The next train headed to Munich won't come through here for days." My heart sank for the second time that morning. I could feel a dark cloud pass over my visage. Pity now shrouded the raven coloured eyes that glanced back toward me in the mirror. "What's your name, dear lady?"

"St. Clare. Cordelia St. Clare." I was so distraught at that point that I didn't even care if some stranger, who might've been motoring us to imminent doom, knew my name.

"Well, Miss St. Clare, I always say..." He stopped short, "Did you say St. Clare? I served with a Robert St. Clare back in The War. Don't suppose there's any relation there?"

For a moment, my despair vanished. "My father's name is Robert and he served in The War," my chest puffed up with pride, "in His Majesty's Royal Air Force."

"Yes, YES!" He guffawed, "Good old Robert St. Clare—you couldn't meet a finer chap! I'm from Berkshire and he's from Manchester. Unbelievable." He shook his head, "I had a feeling about you as I saw you in

36

that square—I most certainly did. Something told me, *'Peter, help those young people.'* Your father saved my life, once. I've felt indebted to him ever since."

Victor piped up, "Well, spirit us away to Munich in time to reach the train, and I'm sure he'll consider the debt fully repaid."

A twinkle gleamed in the Commodore's eye. "I don't know about spirits, my boy—unless you're speaking of the liquid variety." He snickered at his little joke, "However, I can do you one better. Tell me, Miss St. Clare, have you or your betrothed ever flown before?"

Victor and I simultaneously tripped over our words. His: "Why no, no I haven't!" and mine: "He is NOT my betrothed!"

Victor cackled as the Commodore mumbled, "Oh, well...apologies, once more. I just assumed. You two certainly act like you're destined to be a married couple."

I redirected the subject before Victor could belt out yet another inappropriate comment, "What exactly do you mean by flown?"

"To take flight, of course, my dear girl—aviation. I happen to be in the possession of an Avro 504 M. She's the only three-seat biplane in existence. They made her just for me, to honour my service, and such. She's a real beauty! Takes me back to my days when I flew a similar version in The War. I take her up when the mood fancies me. If we leave promptly, barring any complications, I will have you to Munich well before oh-hundred hours—at least a full thirty minutes before your train will reach the station." He giggled like a schoolboy, "I do so love flying in darkness. Reminds me of the times that I flew reconnaissance over Germany."

I began to feel sick, " I...I...I don't know about this..."

"Relax, my dear. You are in the most capable of hands. I will get you to Munich with nary a scratch, and, if you are your father's girl, you will have the time of your life in the process. Trust me."

Victor was incredulous. "Why would you do this for us? What do you possibly have to gain?"

The Commodore's voice took on a stern note, "My dear boy—the RAF is a family. We take care of our own. And, as far as personal gain goes, if you hadn't already noticed, The War left me rather well to do. I have all that I need, and more. Of course I do my duty, but I live my life mostly for sport, now." He mused, almost to himself, "Funny how wars change opinions and behaviours, in that regard."

Rejoining us in the present, his voice took on a lighter tone, "It's settled, then, young people! We will be arriving at my farm soon. It's just on the out-skirts of Strasbourg proper." He chuckled, "You might find it a bit odd for a chap such as myself to be living full time in France, of all places. But my little parcel was a gift from Prime Minister Clemenceau—for my assistance in a few delicate matters during The War. His gratitude was rather magnanimous, I must say. And I have chickens! Anyhow, thereafter, we will be up, up, and away. Huzzah!"

Victor's voice whispered snarky in my ear, "Let me guess...his farm, it's 'the only one like it in existence.'" I elbowed him in the side, which served to temporarily hush his sarcasm.

"Commodore, I don't quite know what to say. A mere thank you wouldn't come close to sufficing."

His eyes radiated with warmth, "When next you see your father, tell him Peter Portal from Berkshire says his debt has been paid." Turning left onto a gravel country lane, he declared, "Young people, we have arrived."

~*~

The generosity that our host offered surpassed comparison, but with each passing minute, my nerves screamed ever the more loudly. Earlier, the Commodore had referred to the happenings back at the square as madness; no, this plan I had agreed to—this was madness. The cool, late afternoon air wedged itself into my bones. It was a suitable companion to the cold fear that enveloped my heart.

Even Victor shivered, and I wasn't entirely convinced that it was all from the temperature. But the Commodore was about as far from anxious as I was from Budapest. "Young people, away we must go. We've got a train to catch." He snickered again—another poor attempt at humour.

I felt weak in the knees, yet still managed to climb aboard with Victor's assistance. Our seats were positioned in a single-file line within the body of the machine. The Commodore, of course, graced the cockpit, I was seated in the middle, and Victor brought up the rear. I would never admit this aloud, but I wished just this once for Victor to be nearer.

At least the Commodore had provided me with a warm, albeit large, jacket, a bomber hat, and goggles to protect my vision. He glanced over his shoulder and smiled. "Hold on, dear lady. It's time to get this bird up in the air!" He flicked gadgets and gizmos on the instrument panel. The propeller began to spin—slowly at first, then faster and faster.

I looked over my shoulder at Victor, who appeared on the edge of his seat with excitement, rather than with fear. The aeroplane rocketed forward with a lurch. I covered my mouth with one hand to hold in a squeal. I used the other to hold onto my own seat for dear life.

The field that we taxied across was flat and wide open, though well marked, as though this was not the first trip . We picked up speed, which made me cringe even further. It felt as though my body was going to shake apart as the aeroplane began to rise into the air. The Commodore expressed his obvious elation with a loud whoop, and Victor cried out in kind.

My knuckles turned as white as my frock as we climbed higher and higher into the air. Perhaps I wasn't 'my father's girl' after all, as the Commodore had previously suggested. I rapidly gulped for air in an attempt to quell my panic. A soon-to-be sleepy Strasbourg now lay beneath us; only a few electric lights twinkled here and there like the diamonds spoken of in the popular children's nursery rhyme. Still, we ascended. We aviated through a bank of clouds, which surprisingly felt nothing at all like cotton, then the aeroplane finally levelled off.

We flew for hours. My only respite had come straight away, from witnessing a breathtaking sunset as we crossed over the Rhine. Victor and I both craned our necks behind us to survey the splendour. The Rhine literally glowed. At such a height, it felt as though we were one with the fabric of the sun.  For a brief moment, I completely desensitized myself to the displeasure of the journey and basked in the luminescence. All too soon, though, I crash landed back down to reality. My derriere was, indeed, asleep.

I fidgeted in my seat and attempted to provide myself with a little relief. Meanwhile, Victor dozed behind me with his chin glued to his chest. I couldn't rest, as my nerves were quite shot. I now understood why the Black Forest gained its namesake. The oppressive canopy of evergreens looming below us along the forest floor brought about a sense of foreboding in the pit of my stomach. From above, in the almost full darkness, it appeared almost impenetrable.

The Commodore checked over his shoulder, then once more. Curious, I did the same. Another aeroplane followed, and closer than I cared for. The machine was bearing down on us at an alarming rate. Aggravation was etched across the set of the Commodore's shoulders. He did yet another double take. Without warning, something whizzed by our aeroplane…then again, and again. The Commodore shouted, "What the bloody hell?" Our machine shuddered in a way that could only be due to an impact. We had been struck! The plane that so closely followed was shooting at us!

The Commodore spoke into his radio, and I barely caught the words, "Mayday, mayday…" before my heart once more seized with panic. Smoke billowed from somewhere underneath our aeroplane, and we jerkily began to descend. I screamed.

Victor, finally roused from his slumber, shuddered, wide-eyed and instantly on the alert. He mimicked the Commodore's earlier sentiment, "What the bloody hell?"

The Commodore shouted, "Hold on, young people! This could get bumpy!" As we hurtled toward the ground, I couldn't help myself. I fainted

41

# Munich—1936

# Chapter 6
## Victor

I reclined on my back and looked up at a night sky blanketed with stars. Momentarily, I was taken back to a childhood long over. But a splinter of a thought nagged at the edge of my subconscious. It interrupted my peace. Cordelia. In an instant, previous events rushed back: shots whizzing past from behind, smoke from beneath, the nosedive, immense pain, and then blackness. My dream had become a nightmare. "CORDELIA?" I shouted.

My limbs shook, yet somehow I pulled myself up to a somewhat seated position and surveyed the scene. I had a tough time discerning between shadows and reality. Smoke continued to bilge forth from the underbelly of the plane. I barely recognized the disfigured machine that now rested in pieces in front of me.

As I rose to my feet, I felt dazed. My balance was beyond muddled. I fought a wave of nausea, but quickly regained composure. For the first time in my life, I wasn't focused on my own well-being. I dashed toward the plane as best as I could. Debris littered the ground before me.

The main body of the craft appeared mostly in one piece. Somehow, even the cockpit lights were still running. Upon arrival there, I made an unsettling discovery. Peter had passed. He now flew with feathered wings instead of mechanical ones. For all of his bravery, for all of his mercy, for all of his kindness, he had perished, all the same.

I couldn't help but feel guilty. Though not through intention, we had aided in his demise. Had we never accepted his offer of assistance, his death would not have occurred. He would've probably been sleeping soundly in his farmhouse—dreaming of tooling about town in his beloved motorcar or sharing his role in some wartime adventure with another complete stranger. My heart grew heavier by the second.

A smile had etched itself upon Peter's inanimate face. Knowing him as little as I did, I still felt that this was how he would have wanted to go. "Goodbye old chap," I muttered as I fashioned an awkward salute, "your last adventure may not have been your greatest, but it was certainly appreciated, nonetheless."

I had enough wits about me to grab an electric torch from the cockpit. Cordelia was nowhere to be seen. Further inspection of the aeroplane evinced that her buckle had broken. I could only assume that she had been thrown from the craft as I had.

I moved back to my own seat. There under it, and in as pristine a condition as if we had gently landed on an airstrip, sat my bag. I howled in disbelief—tinged with a bit of madness—and dropped it to the ground beside me. I surveyed the scene once more for Cordelia. Nothing. A cocktail of bile and panic rose in my throat.

A fit of coughing wracked from the tall grass behind me. Cordelia! I rushed to her side. She was covered in dirt, and her goggles sat cracked and askew on her lovely face. A trickle of blood ran down her cheek, and her blue eyes were bewildered. But she was safe..

I let out a sigh of relief. After all, I couldn't deal with her death on my conscience, as well, I told myself. I almost had myself convinced that was the reason for my joy at discovering her unharmed. Almost. Even though her clothes were torn, and she was covered in muck, she still looked wonderful. *Damn it, Victor, stay focused.*

"Victor? Wh...where are we? What happened?"

44

I gently assisted her to a seated position. "Cordy, you've got to take it easy." No sooner than those words had escaped from my lips, she spotted Peter slumped and unmoving in the cockpit.

A look of horror settled on her face, "Peter? PETER..." she cried. She struggled to her feet and careened toward him. I intercepted her and caught her as she fell to her knees from grief and exhaustion.

"No, no, no, Cordy! You don't need to see him like that."

She burst into tears. "This is all your fault," she bawled, "The bags, Forte, missing the train, Peter!" She beat her fists against my chest.

"I know, I know." It was all that I could muster. She was right. If I hadn't mixed up our bags in Paris, none of this would have happened. My profession and my devil-may-care attitude toward life had now caused someone to lose theirs, and nearly ended Cordelia's in the process.

Though she was still deeply mired in grief, I helped her to her feet. What I assumed to be Munich lay on the horizon, and I knew that we needed to reach the city as quickly as possible. "Cordy," I began.

"Don't call me CORDY," she shrieked.

"Cordelia," I softly backtracked, "we have to keep moving."

"But what about Peter? We can't just leave him here like...like this," she whispered through her tears.

"I know, darling, trust me—I don't want to either. But we can't stay. Despite what has happened, you need to get to that train, and I need to get away from Forte. I know this was his doing, and he'll be searching for the wreckage soon enough. Too soon. Cordelia..." I paused. "We're so close. Peter wouldn't have wanted the loss of his life to have been for nothing."

"But leaving him feels so wrong." Her grief threatened to take complete hold of her once more. I gripped her shoulders and forced her to focus on my words.

"The smoke from the aeroplane will be visible. Someone will come to assist as soon as they see it. I promise." It was clear that Cordelia didn't like the idea, but she consented. Together, we limped forward toward the city. We had no choice.

~*~

When I thought that we would both drop from weariness, we crested the final hill. Below us lay Munich—God be praised. Peter had done us proud. Cordelia had barely spoken during the lengthy walk. Unlike in Strasbourg, on this excursion the silence was palpable. A number of times, I had to take her hand to gently, but firmly, pull her along. The shock from Peter's death was immense, and her focus was all but obliterated.

My first objective, upon reaching the city proper, was to procure us food and drink. Perhaps this would serve to break Cordelia from her current state of stupor. Fortune smiled down upon us as we happened across a *biergarten,* the *Hofbräuhaus,* tucked into a snug little corner. I will admit, I felt no affinity toward the large flag, adorned with its equally large swastika, hanging above the doorway. It looked like a menacing black spider, and it gave me the bloody creeps. But we needed nourishment, and the fact that I didn't appreciate the decor took little away from that. I steered Cordelia inside.

The establishment was most difficult to navigate, crowded as it were to the point of claustrophobia with men in uniform. Spying the only empty table,

I pulled Cordelia toward it. In doing so, I brushed shoulders with one of the uniformed men standing within close proximity to us. He wore the markings of one high in command. "Pardon me, chap," I uttered.

The man stared me down with suspicion. His dark, rectangular moustache twitched, as in frustration. I grinned, rather sheepishly, to cover my awkward embarrassment. This man gave me the creeps worse than the flag outside of the establishment had. Despite my inner aversion to the officer, I enquired the time of him in broken German.

"*Es ist elf Uhr drei*β*ig,*" he coldly replied before he turned on his heel and clipped away at a brisk pace. Eleven thirty in the evening. Well done again, Peter. Even with our journey on foot, we had arrived in Munich a full hour before the train was set to depart.

Honey coloured lager was delivered to the table. Cordelia settled into the corner booth, her lips not saying anything, but her watering eyes saying everything. Eyeing her and myself, I realized that we would both require a change of clothes, at the very least. I dared not ask her size. Doing so, even under normal circumstances, would risk bringing out the woman's wrath. And our circumstances were far from normal. I would simply have to guess.

"Cordy," I began, but the look of disgust I received halted me dead in my tracks. "Cordelia," I tried again, "I'm going to find us a change of clothes for the train. I'll be back as soon as possible, and we'll head to the station, straight away." I spoke to her as one would to a frightened child—both loudly and slowly.

Anxiety flashed across her face as she reached across the table for my hand, "You will hurry, won't you Victor?"

"Of course I will, Cordy— damn it—Cordelia. I'm sorry." I flushed, from my embarrassment, the after effects of the beer, or from her touch, I couldn't say. "I will be back before you know it." Her face dimly lit with a wan smile. Leaving her in that *biergarten* was bloody difficult. But she needed the rest, and we needed the provisions. A chap had to do what a chap had to do.

I wandered for a few moments, taking in the unfamiliar city, as I briskly searched for my destination. It wasn't like Paris or even Strasbourg. Few people were milling about this late in the evening, and those who were seemed glum and suspicious. Fear pervaded the air. I felt worse by the moment.

Thankfully, before long, I found a shop that sold clothing. It was closed and locked up tight, but clearly no match for my skills. I skirted the building and quickly picked the lock on the back door. I utilized the electric torch yet again and chose a plain, yet pretty, dress for Cordelia. It looked to be about her size, and even in my haste, I noticed that its fabric mimicked the colour of her eyes. For myself, I grabbed a pair of rugged brown trousers, a chequered, button-down shirt, and a cap.

I glanced in the mirror after changing. I looked like a farmer, but at the moment, it didn't even matter. I left what I felt to be an appropriate amount of money on the counter to cover the cost of the clothing, and left the way that I came in. I disposed of my former rags in a random outdoor trash receptacle and moved on to my next errand. I wanted to get back to the *biergarten* as quickly as possible.

Perhaps my get up would disguise me from Forte. Just the thought of him sent shivers down my spine. I glanced nervously over my shoulder, expecting him to be standing behind me or nearby in the shadows. He was neither.

This provided little comfort and only served to darken my mood that much further. He would resurface. Of that fact, I had no doubt.

I shoved my fear aside, and rather focused on provisions. A small, neighbouring shop afforded me a loaf of bread, a couple of apples, and some cheese. I entered it in much the same way as the clothing shop, and again, I left an appropriate amount of money on the counter before I cleared out. I shook my head. I had never done anything like this before. I was accustomed to taking what I needed without a pang of guilt. How and why had this changed?

With my purchases and my case in tow, I rushed back to the *biergarten* and Cordelia. Call it my thief's intuition, but something felt off to me. With stealth, I made my way through the door, around the crowd, and toward our corner. My stomach lurched into my throat. Cordelia was not alone.

Across from her sat a wiry gentleman. His back was to me, but his profile suggested glasses and a thick brown moustache. A policeman's cap lay on the table in front of him. He was older than me by some years, but I felt certain that he would pose a fair challenge..

I pulled my cap down snugly and crept closer to them, but kept myself hidden behind the masses of uniformed men. I leaned covertly against the post that framed our booth. I could hear him speaking to her in earnest, "You see, *Fraulein*, this Victor, as you know him, has been a nuisance to us at The Yard for a very long time. He makes acquaintances with some rather shady characters."

Cordelia rolled her eyes. Her spirit had obviously revived. "Although my dishevelled countenance may cause you to think otherwise, I am no *Fraulein*." Her stare was bold, "I am barely acquainted with Victor. Circumstances have seemingly bound us together as of late, but there is nothing more to the matter."

He bowed his head slightly in acquiescence and continued without missing a beat, "Apologies, *Mademoiselle*. We have attempted to capture Victor, but he has evaded us on countless occasions. He's a petty thief, at best, and honestly not worth his salt to us on his own. However, his connections—especially his latest acquaintance, a man known by the name of Forte—now that's a different story altogether!"

"He must be worth his salt enough, if your previous attempts at his capture have proven so unsuccessful, *oui?*" She shot him a severe glance.

"*Touché*, my dear."

"And, as far as this Forte is concerned, do not speak that name in my presence, *Monsieur*."

"Then you've heard of him, I take it?"

"Much more than that. I wish to have nothing more to do with him, I assure you."

"He's a bad fellow, I won't lie. He's one of the worst sorts, in fact—a man without a conscience who brings about misery to the populace for pure sport. Wouldn't you feel much safer knowing that the likes of him were off the streets for good?"

She assessed him for a moment before speaking, "But, what about Victor?"

"What about him? You said yourself that he meant nothing to you. Circumstances have recently bound the two of you, but they can just as easily unbind you." Cordelia's silence was unnerving to me. The mystery man continued, "All that I would ask of you is that you continue your journey just as you have thus far—in the accompaniment of your 'chaperone.' When the train stops for its brief layover in Vienna, I will be waiting to take Victor into custody. Then, you can be on your way, with my gratitude, and wipe your hands clean of the man."

Somewhere in the *biergarten*, a random patron began singing loudly in German to the tune of "Happy birthday to you." The crowd of officers proceeded to cheer. I barely heard any of it. My mind whirled. None of this made any sense! I wasn't wanted—especially not so much that it would garner international intervention. Why had I gotten myself mixed up with the likes of Forte?

I pulled my cap down even further over my eyes and scanned the floor as the man arose. "Just think about the service that you would be administering to the world, Miss St. Clare. *Enchante, Mademoiselle.*" With that, he flicked a few coins onto the tabletop, turned on his heel, and walked straight past me. I held my breath until he had passed.

What was I to do? I knew that I wasn't Cordelia's favourite person, but surely she wouldn't turn me over to the authorities—especially after I had promised to help her and had made good on that promise to the best of my ability, thus far. Did the adventures that we had shared up until this point mean nothing to her? I thought that she had warmed to me, ever so slightly, since our strange introduction. Was this all an illusion?

As much as the survivalist in me wanted to, though, I couldn't desert her—regardless of her plans. I took a deep breath, then turned the corner with a smile, "Look what I found! Take this into the loo and switch out of those rags."

She actually smiled. "As strange a notion as it is Victor, I get the feeling that you put some thought into this dress." I readied to accept her compliment, but her sarcastic nature came out in full force. "It is obvious that you spent much less consideration on your own apparel." Cordy was back, stinging wit and all.

I gave her a sly grin, "Why, Miss St. Clare! I do believe that your jabbing remarks are in reality a facade for your true feelings."

She laughed once more, "And what would those true feelings be, *Monsieur?*"

"Your words are full of mockery, Mademoiselle, but your eyes tell a different story altogether. They say that I'm looking devilishly handsome."

She chortled, "Oh, really?" With that, she departed for the lavatory. I smiled inwardly. She hadn't disagreed.

My light-heartedness turned to unease with the flip of one of the tabletop's coins. I simply didn't understand. As genuine as our previous moment had felt, she had revealed nothing regarding the gentleman who had been speaking to her. There had been ample opportunity for her to do so. Was she really considering turning me over?

My stomach turned loops. Should I part ways with Cordelia St. Clare here and now and continue on to the train alone? The authorities were looking for me, and I was doubly sure that Forte wasn't far behind. Even still, I could give them all the slip. I had done it before. Alas, too late. Cordelia returned quicker than I had imagined that she would. The smile that graced her face was genuine. I couldn't help but reply in kind.

"What do you think?" she beamed.

"Simply lovely." It was true..

"So, what now?" Her delicate brow furrowed.

I paused. I didn't want to be too direct, but if she had decided to blow the whistle on me, I needed to be aware. Even knowing what I knew, though, I wanted to trust her. If nothing else, I had to make her believe that I did.

"I want to get something out there, as it were," I cleared my throat, unsure of where I was going with the conversation, but continuing anyway. "You see, Cordelia, I know that I'm a bit of a rough around the edges sort of fellow, and not of much use to anyone. This adventure of ours should've never even occurred in the first place. But it has, and it is…and quite frankly, I'm grateful for it. I know that it's had its ups and downs, but through it all, I've come to feel a certain way about you." Her eyes widened, and I coughed,      "Er…what I'm trying to say is that in my line of work you learn to trust no one. But, I trust you, Cordelia St. Clare. And I hope that you trust me." My voice softened, "We will part ways in Vienna. So, I thought that you should at least be made aware."

She stared at me. By her expression, it was clear that she was weighing the idea of whether to divulge her secret conversation to me or not. My heart sank when she simply replied, "Thank you for that, Victor. Of course I trust you."

Damn. I so wanted her to come clean, then and there. But it was not to be. Once we boarded the train and separated to our cabins, I needed to formulate some sort of escape plan for my arrival in Vienna. "Very well," I smiled so as to mask the melancholy that gripped my heart. "Let's go catch this train, shall we?"

# Vienna—1936

# Chapter 7
## Cordelia

Scenery traversed past my window once more. It had been less than one day since I had found respite within this compartment, but it felt as though a lifetime ago. I paced by the window, and my mind raced to rival the pace of the train.

The Inspector, as he had referred to himself, had left my thoughts in a quandary. Typically, I could see the black and white contrast of any situation, but at this moment, I was fraught with indecision. Victor wasn't a bad sort. My woman's intuition told me so. Misguided, yes. A rapscallion, absolutely. But bad, not at all.

How he had gotten himself mixed up with someone as dangerous as Forte, I hadn't a clue. But The Inspector had stated, himself—Victor was no more than a petty thief. Did he deserve hard time for his previous actions? Would our recent run-ins with Forte scare Victor straight?

"Cordelia Rose St. Clare, what are you thinking?" I muttered aloud. "He's a thief. He steals—for a living, no less He could have an honest, upstanding profession, yet he chooses not to. He knows what he does, and yet he does it anyway." My mind rationalized outstanding points. Even so, my heart was not entirely convinced. I uttered an exasperated sigh.

For the better part of the hour, conversations between my two halves drug on. What was wrong with me? I barely even knew Victor, so why was my heart enkindled in such a manner? Be it the adventure, or even his annoying charm, I wasn't sure. All I did know was that I had to get back to my senses.

Besides, turning him over to The Inspector might do Victor a world of good. It was my civic duty to assist in reforming this man! My mind had been made up. When The Inspector moved to take custody of him in Vienna, I would do nothing. I might even avoid the scene entirely, and wait here in my compartment. It was the right thing to do. So, why did the decision feel so wrong?

I slumped onto my sofa in thorough exhaustion. In the past day, I had taken part in enough escapades to pen an adventure story of my very own. I fell into a fitful sleep. Victor's face—wearing that innocent-eyed look as he bared his soul to me in the *biergarten*—pervaded my dreams.

The train's shrill whistle shocked me to my feet. I had dozed away the remaining hours of the journey. Victor. What did I do? What was to become of him? I simply had to know. I rushed out the door of my compartment. I knocked on the door of his, but to no avail. No response. Down the corridor, toward the exit, the hallway jammed with departing passengers. I nervously scanned the crowd. Victor was nowhere within view.

I became ensnared in the horde and was herded along at their bovine pace. The awaiting platform was so close, yet still so far. The Inspector, along with three other men of the law, stood there in wait. His stare was as piercing as the train whistle had been. Still, Victor was nowhere to be seen.

I made my way onto the platform and out of the claustrophobia of the departing crowd. The Inspector eyed me suspiciously. "Ahhh, *Mademoiselle*. Fancy meeting you here, and such a shame that we haven't become properly introduced to your previous traveling companion as of yet. There wouldn't be a particular reason for that, now would there?"

"I could not pretend to know what you are inferring, *Monsieur*."

"It's rather simple. I'll spell it out for you, my dear. I'm thinking that you had a change of heart sometime since last we spoke and alerted Victor to my plan."

"Don't be absurd!" One of the porters from the train brushed against me. I was so infuriated that I barely paid attention to his mumbled pardon. "Why would I do such a thing?"

"That is equally simple, Miss St. Clare. You've taken quite the shine to him. It was written all over your face and your tone of voice in Munich." I clenched my fists as he continued—partially because he had enraged me and partially because he had hit the mark. He continued, "I see it all the time in my line of work—innocent ladies such as yourself becoming infatuated with lads who display such roguish charm. You all think, *but I can change him,*'" the girlish tone of his voice angered me even further. His voice darkened, "Truth be told, there is no changing the likes of a thief. The thrill—it courses through their veins, stronger than blood."

He shook his head sympathetically. "I had such high hopes for you. You seemed like such an intelligent young woman. Ah well, no matter..." he nodded his head to the uniformed man on his left, "Restrain her, would you?"

I spluttered, "Excuse me? How dare you?"

He chuckled, "Maybe you're not as intelligent as I originally thought, Miss St. Clare. Victor has stuck with you this long, so that tells me that he's taken quite the shine to you, as well. I completely understand—I do—you're a lovely young woman! Do you really think that he'll allow you to be incarcerated in his stead without at least attempting to rescue you?"

My eyes blazed blue fire. "You're wrong. He won't attempt to rescue me. He doesn't care about me in the least."

"That's where you're wrong..." The words buzzed against my ear. They were spoken from the porter who had brushed against me moments previously. But he wasn't just any ordinary porter. Victor stood behind me—outfitted as he had been yesterday morning when I jerked him into my compartment.

He punched the face of the officer that was holding onto me. His punch must have packed quite the wallop, because the officer's grasp loosened enough for Victor to pull me free. For the second time in two days, he yelled, "Cordelia—RUN!"

We instinctively grabbed onto one another and shoved our way through the crowd. The Inspector drew his weapon and thundered, "Stop them! Stop them, I say, in the name of the law!" The crowd appeared to be shocked into lethargy.

One burly looking type tried to grasp me, but I slapped him with all of the force that I could muster. My free hand stung and the man looked dazed. "Way to go, Cordy! That's the spirit! Oh dear..." Victor lurched forward, pulling me along, as the man shook himself out of his stupor and lunged for us. The Inspector and his men fanned out behind the belligerent fellow. All were right on our heels.

Without warning, the man gripped me. Victor lost his hold as the man wrapped his burly arms around me and pulled me in close. Lightning-quick, he brought a switchblade to my throat. I squeezed my eyes shut. Tears began to well and spill out of their corners. Victor uttered, "Cordelia, don't be alarmed. Just do as the man says. Do you hear me? Just do as the man says."

The lunatic shouted to the officers and to the crowd, "Don't anybody come any closer or I'll slit her throat. I'll do it...I mean it! Now back up!" The officers looked to the Inspector for guidance. They did not move quickly enough for the man's liking. "I said, BACK UP!" He muttered toward Victor out of the corner of his mouth, "Keep close, laddy."

"You don't want to do this," the Inspector spoke calmly. "My quarrel is not with you, sir. Let her go, walk away, and allow my men to do their jobs."

"How's about you spend less time telling me what I want to do and more time BACKING UP...or so help me, I'll cut her!" I whimpered as the knife-edge dug into my flesh a little more closely than I cared for.

"All right, all right...just calm down. Let's talk this through," the Inspector placated as the man began dragging me backward through part of the crowd and toward a nearby alley. Victor kept pace with the man and withdrew, as well. Just as quickly as he had seized me, the unknown man jerked the knife away from my throat and shoved me toward the alley.

"Run like the devil nipped at your heels, lass!" he yelled. Natural instinct took hold, and I complied. We three dashed into the alley. A bullet whizzed past and buried into the wall just behind us. I ran just like my captor suggested, because the devil truly was at my heels—with a bit of space in between, thanks to the crowd.

My captor took the lead and ducked into a grimy, partially hidden doorway near the middle of the alley. The stairwell just inside of it was dimly lit and smelled of heartache and urine. Victor and my captor used their bodies to barricade the door. The man placed his finger against my lips to shush me.

I held my breath and covered my mouth with both hands for good measure. I felt as though my heart were going to explode. I could hear figures rush past the doorway and, I assumed, out the other side of the alley. I knew that at least one of these was the Inspector.

We waited for what felt to be an eternity before Victor and my captor loosened their force against the doorway. I finally felt comfortable enough to take a deep breath. Victor and the man began to laugh—randomly at first, then loudly guffawing. My captor picked Victor up in a bear hug.

"I'm always getting your bloody arse out of a pinch, but this time was nothing like that job we pulled off in London, right laddy? What the bloody hell are you doing in Vienna?" My jaw dropped as the man clapped Victor on the back.

"No, what are YOU doing in Vienna?" Victor voiced the words between bouts of laughter. But the laughter ceased and his words stumbled all over themselves as his glance fell on my puzzled countenance, "Er, hold up, Cordy. Let me explain...Cordelia St. Clare, meet my long time friend and lock picker extraordinaire, Angus Worthington."

"Ex-lock picker extraordinaire. I've quit the business. Gone all respectable like...even found myself a lass of m'own and fathered some bairns. So there's the answer to your question." He nodded his head, "The pleasure is all mine, lass. Sorry about the rough treatment earlier." My jaw felt permanently unhinged. Angus laughed once more, "I think your lady's lost her tongue."

I finally could speak, "I'm not his...oh, ugh, never mind... What in the world is going on?"

"God Himself has sent one of his angels to rescue us—that's what's going on, Cordy!" Victor laughed once more. Even being the slighter man, he proceeded to place Angus in a headlock. I laughed in spite of myself, partially from relief and partially at his antics. Angus, who appeared to be more teddy bear than knife wielding lock picker, momentarily allowed Victor to wallow him.

After their roughhousing finally culminated, Angus queried, "Are you here on a job, Victor?" He paused and then answered himself out loud. "Of course you are...you're always on a job."

Victor smiled, "You know me too well, my friend."

"Got your lady friend here working up some action, too, I take it?"

"No, not at all," Victor looked at the ground, clearly embarrassed. "Cordelia keeps getting caught up in my little 'adventure,' if you will." His voice grew soft. "I've really bungled things for her this time."

I spoke confidently, "We'll manage. We have thus far. Bring on the adventure, I always say."

Victor was astonished, "You've never once said that, Cordelia St. Clare!"

~*~

We bade fond farewells to Angus and left him to resume his original journey. He had stuck out his neck for us, yet we didn't want to place an even larger target on his back by employing him any further. We both knew that heading back toward the train was not an option. Time had seemed to stand still during our escapade, but it truly stands still for none. The train was probably well on its way, and by now, the station was certainly crawling with the authorities. Panic clenched my gut. How would I make it to Budapest?

It was like Victor had read my mind. "Cordelia, we're in an even bigger mess than we were before, and again, it's all my fault. But, I promise you—I will not let you down. You will make it to your employer in Budapest. I will see to that."

"You haven't let me down, yet, Victor. Not once."

"But…"

"But nothing! Victor, you rescued me back there—and in Munich. You could've walked away and never once looked back, but you didn't. I'm forever in your debt."

"You would've done the same for me, Cordelia."

"How do you know? Victor! I almost aided the Inspector in your capture. At the very last minute, my heart changed my mind for me, and I rushed onto that platform to assist you if I could. But, what if I hadn't listened to my heart? I just as easily could've not changed my mind. Victor, I…I…" my voice broke.

"Shhh—but you did," Victor's tone was gentle, "That's what counts. You did." He pulled me into his arms. Both safety and comfort emanated from his every pore. Was something even deeper floating there in the air between us, as well? I leaned my head away from the arch of his neck and searched his eyes…really searched them. Yesterday morning, as I did the same, I felt entirely different emotions. It's amazing how circumstance can completely derail all of your preconceived notions.

# Chapter 8
## Cordelia

I broke from Victor's embrace. "What do we do now? We need a plan of action."

"*We* won't be doing anything. I will be escorting you onto another train before I go to conduct my business."

"Victor, you know perfectly well that the train station is heavily monitored by now. Besides, who knows when the next train to Budapest makes a stop in Vienna? It could be hours—days, even. We have no other modes of transport hiding up our sleeves, and either the Inspector or Forte—or both—could turn up around any bend."

"Well then, what do you suggest?"

"We need to stick together. You could conduct your business and then perhaps we could...borrow a car and transport me to Budapest."

"And by 'borrow,' you mean steal? Why, Cordelia St. Clare! I'm both shocked and appalled at the suggestion!"

I rolled my eyes at his humour, "Says the man ready to fence a 'borrowed' necklace. How rich."

"That's what you'll be saying after I conduct my business, poppet."
I shook my head and sighed. That man. Victor's brow furrowed, "Your plan just might work, but it means we will have to lay low for the rest of the day. I won't be meeting my connection until later this evening."

"Where will you be meeting this connection?"

"Outside the Lower Belvedere...in the gardens, to be exact. Some sort of masquerade ball is going on there tonight. My connection represents an important connection of his own, or so I've been told."

"Ahhh, so you were once the middle man, and now your connection is the middle man? How complex!"

"Yes." His gaze turned sly, "You know, for someone so green, you're quite astute. Are you certain that you're as innocent as you're giving yourself credit?"

I chuckled, "I've read many mysteries. Gatsby isn't the only favourite of mine. If you must know, one easily picks up on the lingo." A dreamy notion stirred deeply within and crossed my face, despite my best efforts to conceal it.

"What was that look for?"

"Excuse me?"

"That look...you know..." A ridiculous expression crossed his face and he sighed dramatically.

I laughed out loud, "Well I hope that I didn't express quite that particular look." My lightheartedness was contagious. It felt good—almost cathartic—to laugh together in such a silly way. Our adventures had begun to take their toll on each of us for certain.

We slowly regained our composure, however Victor's curiosity would not be quelled. "Well, have it out."

I felt my cheeks flame, "I don't know. A masquerade sounds rather lovely. I've always wanted to attend a ball...or a party...some sort of frivolous function. To dress up and to dance would be incredibly..."

"Pretentious?"

"I was going to say romantic, you sod."

"Ahh, yes—romantic." A calculating expression passed across his face. "Cordelia?"

"Hmmm?"

"Do you remember what I told you in your compartment yesterday—as I was stretched out across your floor?"

"You verbalized so much. I need specifics."

His eyes twinkled, "I told you that my trinket would look lovely on you because you had the bone structure for it..."

"Yes—and somewhere in there you insulted my dress, if I recall correctly."

"Apologies, *ma chérie*. But, that dress was all wrong...this one is, too."

"What? I beg your pardon—you picked this one out yourself!"

His eyes twinkled with mischief as he spoke, "Cordy, I think we need to do some more borrowing."

~*~

I felt caught up in a dream from which I prayed I wouldn't awaken. We spent the better part of the afternoon ducking down alleyways and looking over our shoulders. When we happened across a posh clothing shop, we gladly rushed inside.

The shopkeeper turned his nose up at our dishevelled appearances—until Victor began flashing pound notes. Suddenly, we became his top priority. He treated us to an extravagant tea and allowed us to try on practically everything in his shop. I felt like a little girl in the world's largest dress up closet.

After we both made our selections—mine, a classic red number and Victor's, an even more classic black tuxedo with tails—stylists appeared at the snap of the shopkeeper's fingers. They whisked us off to separate dressing areas. At the capable hands of my stylist, I was transformed from an ugly duckling into a graceful swan.

My hair was intricately coiled, which all the more highlighted the bone structure Victor had previously complimented. The deep crimson hue of my gown made my pale skin glow and the blue of my eyes sparkle. Both the delicate straps of the gown and its deeply plunging back were steps away from scandalous. I had never shown this much skin before.

I emerged from the dressing area to find Victor leaned against the wall. I almost didn't recognize him; he looked beyond dapper—like Jay Gatsby. He'd been freshly shaved and his dark hair was parted and slicked. The ebony of his eyes shone like melted dark chocolate when his glance landed upon me.

He didn't speak—only stared—but his wordless state expressed volumes. I blushed as deeply crimson as my gown. This brought him to his senses. He cleared his throat, and then he softly proclaimed, "Cordelia—you look lovely," he sauntered toward me, "but you need this." He reached around to the back of my neck. I closed my eyes and breathed in his aftershave as he clasped the necklace.

He spun me around to face the full-length mirror that hung on the wall behind me. My mouth dropped as I took in the image. We appeared to be two completely different people. We were two completely different people—at least, I certainly had changed. Gone was the shy, proper, frumpy girl from yesterday. She had been replaced by a courageous—dare I say beautiful—worldly woman.

The shopkeeper hailed a luxurious cab, and smiled as he walked away with the majority of Victor's money. I felt guilty due to the whole affair and attempted to protest, but Victor shushed me. "Seeing you in that dress makes it all worth it." My heart skipped a beat.

The lights of the Belvedere glowed star-like and rivalled even Van Gogh's brush strokes. I was in awe at such splendour until Victor's voice buzzed, once more, in my ear, "Don't forget your masque, poppet." I donned a feathered red masque, while Victor's sleek black one complemented his elegant suit.

The coat check girl's face flashed confusion as Victor handed her his dowdy bag, but she graciously accepted it, nonetheless. Hushed conversation flowed as readily as bubbly champagne. We each acquired a glass and clinked them together in a silent toast. Victor snapped open an antique pocket watch to check the time. I couldn't help but comment, "How lovely. Did you procure this back at the shop?"

"Actually, no. I've had this for years. It was one of the first things that I pinched in my younger days. I saw it hanging from a gentleman's waistcoat, and I wanted it more than anything else in the world." He glanced around, " I never would've imagined then that I would be found in some place like this, now," he cleared his throat, "with someone like you."

"I don't know if I should take that as a compliment or not." I smiled.

He grinned, "Yes, yes you should." A troubled look passed across his face. Even despite the concealment of his masque, it showed through in his eyes, "Even though this is a fairy tale, I'm allowing myself to believe that it's real—for just one night. We can travel back to reality in the morning."

"Oh, Victor..."

He glanced away as he continued speaking, and his voice was fraught with emotion, "You deserve to own a necklace like that, Cordelia. You should have a jewelry box full of them, and a closet stuffed with fancy gowns, too. Someone respectable, like any of the other gents in here, could provide you with those sorts of things."

I attempted to lighten his mood, "Whatever would I do with all of that? Give me shelves full of books, instead."

The gaze that met my own was intense, "I would like to. I would like to give you the world on a string." His eyes held mine under lock and key. I was helplessly ensnared. My mouth opened, but just as the words of my heart began to bubble forth like a fountain, a gentleman grasped Victor's arm and broke the spell.

"*Monsieur Marceau*, I presume?"

Victor's eyes flashed recognition at the name. He remained aloof, though. "That depends on who wishes to know. You are?"

The stranger smiled and spoke in a jovial tone. The rest of the room would have presumed that he was simply making conversation, but his words were slicing, " You know very well who I am. You were supposed to meet me in the gardens—alone."

"Ahh, yes—well, apologies, sir. There was a slight change in plans. We were actually just heading in that direction." He paused, "How did you recognize me, again?"

"My employer noticed the necklace, as well as the lady wearing it. He now wishes to make acquaintance with both before dispensing compensation."

"I think not. Your employer would be wise to stick to the original deal and leave the lady out of it."

"Had you met me alone and in the gardens as we had scheduled, the original deal would have taken place. Now, a new deal is in effect. Congratulate yourself for it, or be on your way."

Victor's chest heaved. I interrupted before he could anger the stranger even further than he obviously already had. "Vic—er, *Monsieur Marceau*, calm yourself." I held my head high. "Show me the way to your employer, sir."

"Cordelia—you don't have to do this. You've been involved in far too much, already."

"Will you excuse us for a moment?" I didn't give the stranger time to respond. Instead, I pulled Victor a few feet away, "Victor! This has been your goal all along. Would you please relax and allow me to be of assistance?"

Before Victor could protest, I sashayed back over to the stranger and took his elbow. We walked deeper into the grand hall. My nerves were in full swing as we strolled toward the opposite end of the room, yet I attempted to appear completely collected. "We haven't yet had the pleasure. You would be...?"

"You may call me Tommy."

"Ahh, yes, charmed. I am..." I paused, "Daisy. Daisy Buchanan. And how should I address your employer?" If he heard Victor speak my actual name or recognized my pseudonym, he did not comment, but continued speaking, all business.

"You may call him Edward."

We paused in front of another well-dressed, fair-haired gentleman. He wore an entitled expression—it showed through even underneath his lavish mask. His coldly penetrating eyes swept over me. They lingered upon the necklace for a brief moment before continuing on with their assessment of my figure. With breath accented by liquor as well as The King's English, he spoke, "Stunning. And the necklace isn't half bad either."

As the gentleman and I conversed, I searched the crowd for Victor. With time, I spied him gazing intently down upon us from above, as he leaned upon the second level balcony.. His eyes held none of their former warmth. Edward spoke of his service in The War, as well as his American friend, Wallis, for whom he was procuring the necklace. When asked about his profession, he eluded the question by stating that he held many kingly responsibilities, none of which he particularly enjoyed. I didn't understand his intonation, but as I really didn't care, I didn't press the issue.

Vibrant music sprang forth from the orchestra, and masqued couples looped and swished across the floor. The vision was breathtaking. A bright smile flickered across my lips. Edward noticed this. Even though he appeared to be quite aloof, he obviously paid careful attention to finer details. "Would you care to dance, Ms. Buchanan?"

"I...I...don't dance."

"I'll be the judge of that. Follow my lead." He grasped my arm and pulled me toward the dance floor. I began to panic. As much as a part of me wanted to give in to the romance of it all, some deep intrinsic voice shouted NO. I looked toward the balcony and met Victor's all-too-intense stare.

Victor rushed toward the staircase that led to the dance floor below. He flew down the stairs and nimbly wove his way through the crowd. Reaching Edward and me, he stiffly bowed. "Please allow me to cut in, sir."

An arrogant sneer curled Edward's lip, but he bowed in return, and acquiesced. A rousing Viennese waltz floated through the air. The dancers twirled along to the melody. Victor grasped my hand and led me to the centre of the floor. All of my inhibitions and fears vanished in that moment. They were replaced with pure joy.

It was obvious that neither of us knew what we were doing, but that was of little consequence. We twirled in unison, Victor and I, and it was as if the rest of the assembly disappeared. All that remained was the rhythm of the music and that of our heartbeats. We smiled as though our faces would split apart. When Victor drew me forward for a passionate kiss, this time I did not fight, but eagerly became swept away in the moment.

Our lips finally parted company. Victor stared at me with the exact same expression as he had in my compartment on the train the day before. My stomach fluttered with thousands of butterflies. We had little time to revel, though, as the orchestra screeched to a halt. Tension washed over the room, as a familiar voice boomed. Victor recognized it, as well. The Inspector!

He was looking for us. From across the room, I locked onto Edward's calculating stare. His cold eyes and cold smile were well-suited dance partners. His countenance revealed what my gut already told me to be true: he had alerted the authorities. He seemed to be the type of man who always got what he wanted, and if he did not, his adversary would dearly pay. Victor and I had underestimated this fact. Well, he might have won the battle, but we would win the war!

The Inspector ordered everyone to line up in the centre of the room and remove his or her masques. Edward strode forward, but did not alert the Inspector as to our whereabouts. I was confused, at first, but it dawned upon me that if Edward were to point us out in the crowd, it would implicate him, as well. Victor and I used the movement of the crowd to masque our own escape.

Edward attempted to follow us. His movements weren't as concealed as ours, though. He raised quite the fuss, yet was corralled back into line with the other guests. We slipped into the main foyer, but ducked behind the coat check desk when we noticed that an officer of the law guarded the nearby front entrance.

"Wait here. I'll be right back." Victor crept on all fours into the coat closet. I vehemently whispered, "Victor...no!" When he continued forward, I cringed and attempted to flatten myself against the desk. I knew that I could be discovered at any moment. What felt like an eternity later, Victor re-emerged and tucked what I assumed to be his gun behind his back into the waistband of his pants. We then—through a series of whispers and finger pointing—formulated a plan.

I materialized from behind the desk and stumbled toward the entrance. The officer was brusque, "Stop right there, Miss. You must return to the others at once."

"Oh please, sir—I require fresh air. I'm feeling rather faint. This interrogation is all too much for a woman of my station." I delivered an award winning performance. A character in a novel had made a similar declaration once, and I drew from her dramatics. It worked, as the officer quickly offered his assistance.

Victor crept up behind the officer—as his back was now turned and my theatrics garnered his complete attention. Victor retrieved a nearby vase and bashed the officer across the back of the head. The man fell to the floor in a heap. Victor dragged him to the side of the foyer and out of view.

"Is he dead?" my voice quivered.

"No, but he'll certainly be feeling that in the morning. Now, come on. The others won't be occupied for long."

We ran down the outdoor staircase toward the motorcars that lined the front drive. We jiggled the handles of the nearest parked cars, but all were locked up tight. We then spied one of the empty patrol cars that haphazardly blocked the drive. Its lights were flashing and the driver's door was slightly ajar, as though the driver had rushed onto the scene without properly shutting it. Fortune smiled down upon us even further. Keys were dangling from its ignition. Victor was giddy, "Slide in, Cordelia—hurry!"

I did as I was told, but I voiced my opinion on the matter, "Victor—I don't like this! Not one little bit!"

"Cordelia, we don't have time for anything else." The car roared to life, and Victor whooped. He stepped onto the gas pedal with full force, and the police car sped down the drive with a squeal of its tires.

I glanced back to the entryway of The Belvedere. Officers rushed out of its widely open doorway and down the front stairs. They clambered into the remaining squad cars and gave chase, straightaway. "Victor, hurry, they're gaining on us!" I squealed.

It was as if Victor navigated the streets purely on instinct. I'm still not certain how he accomplished it. Perhaps it was his thief's training—survival at all costs—that kicked into full force. At any rate, when I dared to glance forward, I could see that we were bearing down upon the train station.

The car skidded to a stop and our feet hit the ground at an immediate run. We dashed to the platform as if our very lives depended on reaching a train—any train. An antique railway worker steadily traversed across the platform directly in front of us. Victor almost bowled him over in his full tilt run, but at the last moment, he grasped the man's shoulders and shouted, "Budapest...are any of these trains heading to Budapest?"

The language barrier provided little consequence. Hearing the word Budapest was significant enough. The frightened man pointed a shaky finger toward a freshly departing train. Victor loosened his grasp on the man and transferred his talon-like grip onto my forearm. "Cordelia, come on! We can make it!" We ran, once more, like the devil himself gave chase. The train hadn't quite picked up speed and the conductor was in the process of closing the outer door. "Wait, wait!" Victor implored.

The conductor shook his head, signifying that it was too late, but Victor paid him no heed. He launched the both of us into the doorway and knocked the conductor flat on his back in the process. I felt the fabric of my gown rip in the mid-thigh vicinity, I lost a shoe, and I thought that my arm had been pulled out of its socket, but God be praised, I made it. Victor sheltered me within the crook of his arm and pulled me further into the train.

I had been focused on the task at hand: not being sucked under the body of a moving locomotive. However, in the fraction of time between us fully reaching the interior and Victor sliding the exterior door into place, my attention wavered. I glanced down the body of the train. It provided a momentary snapshot in time, nothing more. But I managed to notice that shadowy figures jumped into other cars down the line in much the same way as we had just done.

The lights of the train station briefly highlighted the jumpers. One in particular's hat resembled that which rested upon the table at the *biergarten* in Munich the previous day. My heart sank at the sight. Admittedly, I was in a heightened state of panic, so perhaps my imagination ran wild. But I could've sworn—as the lights glinted off of the face of another—that he appeared to be wearing a mask made of tin.

*Toward Budapest—1936*

# Chapter Nine
## Victor

All was a blur. After we vaulted over the dazed conductor, we scampered down the hallway. Cordelia had lost a shoe. As she struggled with her lack of footwear and her tattered gown, I attempted to process what had just happened. Whilst surveying our surroundings for danger, I simultaneously pulled her forward. I needed a plan, and I needed it quick.

As we rushed through the carriages, I felt in my gut that Forte was near. Cold, blind fear enveloped my heart. Pausing to look behind us, the only disturbance seemed to be that of a few errant travellers steadying themselves and muttering in disgust at our rude behaviour. Perhaps my fears were unfounded.

Cordelia's words turned my heart to stone, "Victor, the Inspector—he's on the train," she gulped air as she ran, "and so is Forte." The Inspector didn't worry me a stitch. I had evaded sods like him a dozen times or more. But, Forte was a different story entirely.

"What's his plan?" I muttered, more to myself than to her. My mind raced. Perhaps he was hanging back and waiting for us to innocently run into him before snaring us in his trap. He was an arrogant bastard. But he hadn't a clue that we were aware of his presence. Wait a minute—that was it! In that instant my own plan had formed.

Cordelia's face wore a heavy veil of worry. Even so, determination shone in her eyes. She had changed so much in just a short couple of days. No longer was she a stiff. She was brave—much braver than I had ever been. In my profession, I had become accustomed to ducking and running. But not her. She tackled our adventure head on—confidence personified.

I had to don the armour, for her sake, and become the knight errant. I had dragged her into this, now it was time for me to get her out. I would make the final play in this game of cat and mouse. Pulling her to a halt and gripping her by the shoulders, my voice rang, resolute. "Listen to me Cordy—you need to carry on without me."

"No! I won't..." Her eyes shone blue flame. She prepared to lay into me, but I cut her off.

"Yes," I vehemently whispered as I grasped her shoulders, "you WILL! You need to keep going. Get as close to the front as you can and find somewhere to hole up. I will come for you".

"What are you going to do?" Tears began to gather in her eyes. We were both tightly wound and ready to snap.

"I'm going to finish this."

Judging by the way Cordelia looked at me, she wanted to argue against my plan. I could also tell that she knew it would do no good. Somewhere behind us, a gunshot rang out followed by screams of terror. Forte had upped the ante. The time for talking was over. It was time for action.

"Run!" I shouted. Cordelia kicked off her remaining shoe and burst into a sprint. I followed behind—her shadow—but when we reached the carriage parting, I paused. She crossed over to the next carriage and turned. Tears flooded her cheeks, but I refused to follow. At my final shout to go, she sped off down the carriage without me.

Climbing up the ladder leading to the carriage rooftop, I then clambered onto the top of the train. I could hear someone—presumably, Forte—

climbing up the ladder directly behind me. My heart dropped into my shoes as his face appeared, rising out of the darkness. Shadows from the blurred countryside rushed along my left and right sides, but all I could focus upon was his menacing face. Half a sneer and half a tin mask—both illuminated from the full moonlight. He had come for vengeance.

In a short burst, I leapt over his visible head and shoulders, then ducked and scurried along the carriage tops. I hastened down the length of the train, which I had just interiorly traversed, and away from where I presumed Cordelia to be. By some random miracle, I kept my balance. It was a dizzying affair. My stomach weakened with every leap between carriages. Only the buzz from a frenzied rush of adrenaline drove me forward. I counted four carriages left between me and the end of the line. Evading him any longer was hopeless.

I turned. By bending at the knee, I gained a modicum of balance. Forte stopped short a few metres behind me and acquired his own composure. We mentally prepared for war as we each stared the other down with equal disgust. "I don't have the necklace." I shouted above the racket of the train.

Forte's laugh rang out above the din. He bellowed, "I assumed that your contact lay claim to it with no trouble."

"Of course there was no trouble," I bluffed. He needn't know the necklace was still affixed around Cordelia's lovely throat. In all of the confusion after the Inspector stormed the Belvedere, we escaped with the trinket, much to the arrogant Edward's chagrin. The thought made me chuckle, despite my current predicament.

"Well, you've certainly found yourself in trouble at the moment, Victor—make no mistake about that!"

No matter how I calculated, I couldn't work through the different paths this scenario could take with any sort of hope for an escape. My head spun and my footing was unsure. I played one final card. "I've hidden your cut of the money on the train....your original cut plus half from the sale of the necklace." I hoped to appeal to his lust for money.

The moonlight glinted off of his sadistic glare. "This has long since ceased being about money, Victor." His guttural tone caused my insides to tremble. I could initiate a fight, but the odds of me coming out on top were low. He was stronger, by far, and our environment allowed for no mistakes. "It didn't have to happen this way." His teeth bared like those of a rabid dog, "We could have fenced that pretty trifle together, taken our fair shares, and gone our separate ways. But, you had to double-cross me." Cruel laughter rang out, "You will pay for that."

"You're right—about all of it. But, I was afraid that I couldn't trust you." Hope still glimmered, albeit faintly. If I could drag this out, perhaps my instincts would kick in, and I could somehow work out a way to best him.

"Enough talking." He pulled a revolver from his inside jacket pocket. "I'm afraid that this is really going to hurt." He grinned, "Actually, I'm rather glad." He pointed the gun straight at my heart and cocked it.

I refused to watch. I focused over Forte's left shoulder, instead. I prepared myself for impending doom. In doing so, I noticed movement along the railway carriage directly following ours. I squinted. Certainly the stress of my predicament was playing tricks on my eyes. *No, it couldn't be!*

Before he could fire, Forte took stock of my distraction and turned to assess the situation. Two people stumbled along the carriage's body toward us. Cordelia hobbled in the lead. Barefoot, with the tail of her ragged gown thrown over her arm, she wore a grimace. Her hands were raised. A gun, and the man who wielded it, now shadowed her. The Inspector! But, why? He shoved the pistol into her back. Despite her obvious fear, he forced her to leap across the divide to our carriage. He followed suit. By this point, my vision blazed red with anger.

"Look who I found!" the Inspector shouted to Forte. "She was hiding in a first class cupboard. Tsk, tsk—how unladylike".

"Don't you touch her!" I bellowed. None of this made any sense! Were they actually working together? At any rate, our odds were now even worse.

It's a strange feeling when you accept that you are most likely going to die. It begins as a sickness in the pit of your stomach that rises and explodes like a firework and courses through your whole being. Then your mind kicks into play, and you're bathed in numbness. Acceptance washed over me. It was all about Cordelia, now. She didn't deserve to die for me.

"You're late, Inspector." Forte spoke loudly, yet with boredom. It was obvious that he wasn't really bothered by this fact.

"Apologies, old chap. But, look at what else I have." The Inspector pulled Cordelia's hair. She squealed. Moonlight glinted off of the necklace. Forte snarled. He redirected his rage toward me.

"You told me that you got rid of it in Vienna!" Forte spat the words like venom.

"No, actually I never said that. You did. I just didn't disagree with you." Forte's jaw slaked, dumbfounded. The look on the Inspector's face was equally priceless. Even facing certain death, I laughed.

Forte recovered from his shock. A wicked grin spread across the visible half of his face. He turned to face Cordelia, and could I have seen his eyes, I'm sure that they would have pierced holes through her. "Hand over the necklace to me, love, and you won't be harmed."

As the realisation of what was occurring dawned, the bright moonlight highlighted confusion on the Inspector's face. He appeared incredulous, at first. That quickly changed, along with his visage. Despite the shadows, it blazed, quite obviously, a shade of red that would've shamed a rose. I thought that he would explode from the force of the rage that welled up and out of him.

"NO!" He shrieked as he shoved Cordelia behind him. She stumbled backward, dangerously close to the left edge of the roof of the carriage. She righted herself in the nick of time, cowering in a half crouch. The Inspector spluttered, "I led you to him. I kept tabs on them both for you. We were supposed to be equal partners. You promised me my fair share!"

Before any of us could process the movement, Forte shot the Inspector between the eyes. The gun cracked as sparks rivaled the moonlight's luminosity. The Inspector's body slumped backward from the force of the shot. Horrified, Cordelia screamed, landed upon her rump, and scuttled back a few paces, barely dodging his fall. She missed being covered by his dead weight by only a hair's breadth. Her eyes bulged. My heart felt as though it had plunged off of a cliff.

"Well, consider that your share paid in full!" Forte laughed. The side of him that I knew best had surfaced—the maniacal psychopath.

The Inspector's blood gushed from the gaping wound in his skull. A panic stricken Cordelia had obviously never before witnessed anything so gruesome. No one should ever lay claim to such an experience. My mind raced. I had to get to her. "So where do we stand now?" I shouted to gain Forte's attention once more.

"Simple enough. Now, I will kill you. It's such a shame that the lady has to witness this, given the state that she is in. But, as she will be next, she won't have to fret for long."

In my own defense, I assumed a half crouch. Providence, alone, in that very moment caused the train to lurch, knocking Forte's stance off guard. Without even thinking, I sprung forward toward him, targeting his legs. He landed on his back with a surprised, "Oof," as the breath knocked out of him.

My maneuver cost me my tactical advantage. As my legs slid toward the side of the roof, my fingertips screeched along the metal of it for any sort of handhold; I backpedalled, simultaneously, in mid-air for some sort of foothold. I scrambled back atop the rushing train and attempted to right myself. Meanwhile, Forte's daze lasted mere seconds. Cordelia screamed. I dodged, but was immediately met with a left uppercut as he rose to a seated position. The marrying of his fist and my face transpired, a perfect union. I landed upon my posterior, semi-stunned.

Forte loomed larger and much stronger than I. My hope was fuelled only by my speed, yet, at this juncture, proper footwork would prove even more critical. I had to outmaneuver him in order to reach Cordelia. It was time to do what I did best in similar instances—duck, run, and hope for the best. As I had only looked out for one chap—myself—in similar scenarios, I prayed that my strategy could save both Cordelia and me. I shook off the cobwebs from Forte's punch and stood upon the train's pitching terrain. Conditions being as they were, balance was crucial.

Forte still clutched his gun in his right hand. He smacked the butt of it across my forehead, and I fell to my knees, further stupefied. I could hear

Cordelia's fear. It permeated her screams. She became the focus of my attention—my strength—once more. I had to carry on, for her.

Forte dropped to his knees, placed me in a headlock, and whispered in my ear, "I'm going to kill you with haste, and then take my time with the girl. Such a lovely young thing. Ahh, the joy torturing her will bring me. It will make all of this hassle worth it." He laughed. He spun me around and repeatedly punched me in the face. I could taste the iron of fresh blood.

As I pictured him harming Cordelia, rage that I didn't even know existed surged within me. He attempted to hit me again, but this time I grabbed his fist and used it as leverage. I rose to my knees. Surprise crept across the visible half of his face.

His wrist buckled from my weight, as I continued to bear down upon it and find my footing. I towered above him, which inspired a moment of confidence amidst the chaos. I kicked out at his ribs—one last ditch act of strength. He collapsed backward, momentarily winded. In the melee, his gun flew from his hand. It skidded across the slippery rooftop and over the side of the train.

I glanced back at Cordelia, who had grown eerily quiet. Tears streamed down her face, but her gorgeous, cornflower eyes—the very ones that I could swim in from our first, chance encounter—pierced, ice cold. She stood at the Inspector's feet, and the gun in her hands—his gun—pointed straight at Forte. "I assure you, you will not be touching me—or Victor—EVER AGAIN!" she sobbed.

Forte raised himself to a seated position, and brought up both hands, as if in defeat. He assessed me as he wiped blood away from his mouth. Smiling sardonically over his shoulder at Cordelia, he then turned that lunatic grin toward me. At that moment, his plan became obvious. He launched toward me, once again. The fight renewed, more furious than before, as punch after punch was thrown. We tangled in a frenzy of instinct. But I was waning. "SHOOT HIM CORDY," I screamed.

"I CAN'T, VICTOR! I MIGHT HIT YOU," she shouted through her tears.

She was right. So I did the only thing that I could. I wrapped my arms around Forte's chest in a bear hug. His surprise was evident in his gasp. He snarled. Everything was happening so quickly. "DO IT NOW!" I howled as I lurched backward off the side of the train with Forte writhing his protest in my arms. Realization replaced his snarl. A single gunshot permeated the night air, followed by Cordelia's wail of anguish.

It felt as though I fell forever.

*Epilogue*
*Upstate New York—2024*

"I'm desperate for a glass of water. Be a dear, Betsy, and fetch me one, would you?"

Her jaw dropped to her chest, "Now? Right now?"

"Yes, right now. I'm thirsty. I've talked for hours."

"But...but what happened? You can't just leave me hanging like this, Ms. St. Clare! What about Victor...and Forte? Did they die? I need answers!"

"And I need water." Betsy could tell that I wasn't going to budge, so she dashed to the table across the room. The water in the glass that she handed to me was mountain spring cold. I drank heartily. She released a deep breath held from anticipation as I continued.

"There could've been no possible way that they didn't. And I was heartbroken over it. Utterly heartbroken..."

~*~

"*The loneliest moment in someone's life is when they are watching their whole world fall apart, and all they can do is stare blankly.*" *Gatsby* never rang more true than in that very moment. Somehow I managed to crawl to the edge of the roof. I could see nothing, save the tracks illuminated by the light of the cold moon. I prayed that Victor would be hanging off the side, like a scene in an adventure novel. But he was not. I was alone. I had never felt horror like that before. I wouldn't again until another Great War would bring the world once more to its knees. But, we'll save that tale for another day.

I could've died there on top of that train. I'm surprised that I didn't. I clung to the roof in a numb state for minutes—or perhaps hours. I'm uncertain. All I know is at some point, an officer of the law managed to assist me down into the interior of the train. He and his fellow officers had combed the train for the Inspector. When they couldn't find him, they were perplexed.

My rescuer—a keen sort—thought to examine the exterior roof. Luckily, he ascended from the back of the train. Otherwise, I don't know if I would have been within view, or if he would have even scaled its full length, had he climbed from the front as we had. If no one had discovered me until the journey had reached its culmination, I might have very well perished on top of that train.

I managed to share with the officer who I was, as well as to whom I belonged in Budapest, before I blacked out from the trauma of it all. Days later, I awoke in a fluffy white hospital bed with a concerned Dahlia LaRoque at my side. She had stayed there from the moment that she was alerted by the authorities. Upon my waking, we returned together to the family's new home.

I was questioned extensively by the law—multiple times—despite protests from Colonel LaRoque. Eventually, they left me in peace. No one could corroborate my story, the Inspector was dead, and Victor and Forte had been similarly pronounced as such. The Inspector had been considered a top official at The Yard. To have his memory and reputation tainted with such talk would have proven quite scandalous. So, the whole affair was swept under the rug.

"What ever happened to the necklace?"

"Ahhh—bright girl! The necklace. The officers of the law had no idea that it was stolen property. After I awoke, we returned home, and once Lady Dahlia sensed that I was out of the danger zone, she brought it to me. Her gaze burned, questioning,, but she was both wise and discreet. I think I mentioned once before, she was a very liberal woman—quite before her time. Never

88

once did one of those questions pass her lips. I did not volunteer any information, so the matter was never discussed."

"So you kept it?"

"For many years, yes. I hid the necklace under my mattress, for safe-keeping. From time to time, I sneaked it out and wore it—when I was alone with my thoughts. I placed all of the bad from that night in a mental box, sealed it up tight, and shoved it into the farthest corner of my mind's attic. Instead, I chose to focus on all of the good that came from the adventure. I guess I was indeed my father's girl, after all," I winked.

"Sometimes, I would dance a Viennese waltz across my room and remember a masqued young woman in a crimson gown tucked safely in the arms of her fairy-tale prince. Years later, I sold it...when Victor and I needed getaway cash."

"VICTOR?"

I laughed, "Of course, dear. You didn't really think that he was dead, did you?"

"Ummm, YES..."

"Please allow me to explain."

~*~

With each passing day, back then, I grew stronger. Victor would have chalked it up to my stubborn will, I'm sure. The nightmares hung around for longer than I cared to mention, but I kept this fact to myself. I was determined to uphold my duty to the LaRoque family. They could have turned me away,

89

refused my care, or shipped me back to Paris. They did none of these. I owed them my gratitude as well as my life.

Months passed and I acclimated rather nicely to my new environment. One day, after a bit of free time and a lazy walk around Buda Castle and the Castle District, I returned home to discover an unusual package lying upon my bed. It was wrapped in nondescript brown paper, tied with twine, and addressed in a scrawling script. Upon opening it, I almost blacked out from shock.

It was *Gatsby*...my *Gatsby*. I had thought it to be lost in Strasbourg, but Victor had rescued it. Later on, once we were reunited, I discovered that he had placed it in his pocket before he tossed my bag down the alleyway to distract Forte. That's the hands and mind of a thief for you.

Even after the aeroplane crash near Munich, it had miraculously remained in his pocket. And when I assumed that he was clambering for a weapon within his bag in the coat closet in Vienna, he was not only doing so, but was also rescuing the book again. For me—all for me. Tucked inside the book, I found a note. Just a scrap of plain paper with writing in that same scrawl. It read:

*Darling Cordy—*

*It was quite an adventure, wasn't it? For weeks, I've kept watch on you. So many times, I've wanted to reach out to you, but it's been too dangerous for the both of us. Dead men need to remain just that. I'm off—I cannot say where—to reevaluate my life. Perhaps one day, I'll be worthy enough to claim you as my own. Until then, know that I won't be far. You'll be just fine Cordelia St. Clare. Of course, we both already knew that, didn't we?*

*Regards, Monsieur Marceau*

*P.S. I read this—yes, I actually read a book. Stop being snobbish. It was our lucky talisman, so how could I not? Now I understand why it's so dear to your heart.*

Betsy clapped her hands and squealed, "He did survive!"

"Yes, that he did." I smiled. "After they tumbled from atop the train, their positions shifted, mid-air. Forte hit the ground first, and Victor landed upon him. Were it not so, Victor would have perished. For all the harm that he caused, Forte saved Victor's life."

"And your shot, did it hit its mark? Was Victor harmed?"

"My shot rang true. Forte was dead before he ever hit the ground. The bullet grazed Victor's arm, but left merely a scratch. A fact he pointed out on many an occasion, nonetheless." I winked, "I became quite the marksman, as it were, a natural talent. It was a skill that proved rather handy in later escapades."

Betsy grinned. Her queries knew no bounds. "Did Victor ever turn honorable—to *'claim you as his own?'*" She sighed, "It's almost too much...so romantic!"

"It took a while—quite a while. A little over two years to be precise. From time to time, I would receive strange baubles or trinkets, always wrapped in brown paper and signed *'M.M.'* I always knew they were from him. It was silly—the fancy of a young girl's heart—but I waited for him. I turned down many suitors back in the day." I paused to peer out the window at the lengthening, twilight shadows, "None of the others compared."

I cleared my throat. "In 1938, Colonel LaRoque moved the family back to a country house on a tract of land that bordered Paris. This took place before the stage was fully set for the Second World War. After the move, the baubles and trinkets stopped arriving."

Tears brightened Betsy's eyes, "Oh, Ms. St. Clare..."

"Now don't you fret, dear child. That wasn't the last I was to see of my *'Monsieur Marceau,'* never fear. As I mentioned, Lady LaRoque was a rather unconventional woman. We departed for holiday on the loveliest ship in the fall of that year. It turned into quite the romp."

"Was Victor there, too? So there are more stories?" Denise squealed.

"Oh yes, darling, there are always more stories. To quote one who was quite knowledgeable on the subject: *Life is a most extraordinary adventure,'* don't *you know?"*

*The End...or is it?*

# Afterword

I sincerely hope that you enjoyed this adventure. I wrote the sort of story that I would (and did!) love to read; I hope that you fell in love, as well. Every moment that I've spent with Cordelia and Victor has been a pleasure. It's been one of the most joyful writing experiences of my life, thus far.

What started this whole journey for me was elder Cordelia's voice. That last line of the prologue rang as clear as a bell in my head. *"You see, it's about two strangers…and a train."* Shew. I was hooked. Then the rest just flowed. I'm not usually one to outline my stories—I let the stories tell themselves—but this one took off with such a gallop, that I had to take notes. Otherwise, it would've dragged me behind, full speed ahead, literally.

I'm a huge history fan—it's my major—so researching the various auxillary characters, the train and its route, and the cities was a dream. I took an immense amount of time attempting to stay true to the time frame, language, atmosphere, and state of the world, so I hope that all translates. And it was such a blast adding my own spin to the personalities of the characters. If you don't know your history, or even if you do, and if you're so inclined, have fun researching.

This won't be the last you see of Cordelia and Victor, at least, if I have anything to say about it. Their story isn't over quite yet. Life isn't as free wheeling as it once was when I sat every day in the Blacksburg, VA, Starbucks and researched and wrote like the world was on fire. But, someday, I"ll hear Cordelia in my head again, probably scolding me *("What's taking you so long?")*. Then, I will know that the time is at hand.

# Acknolwledgements

This story would not be possible without support from so many.

As always, thanks to God for the beautiful gift of creativity. Thanks, also, to Sir Google, for the vast array of historical knowledge (whiz, bang, kapow) at my fingertips. To Richard Thomas, even though dark, speculative fiction is your wheelhouse, you edited this superbly, and I am beyond grateful. To Denise Baer and Baer Books Press, thank you for yet another wonderful collaboration. To the many friends and family members who have constantly asked, *"When are you going to publish Two Strangers???"* I am grateful for your motivation and your shared love for this little story. To Joshua James, thank you for fleshing out Victor and especially for the epic ballroom scene idea in Vienna. To my wonderful husband, Chad, thank you for always being in my corner. And, always, to you, dear readers. I've said it before, and I'll say it again—you make doing what I do even more fun!

~*~

Until next time, y'all…much love!

## Bio

Jennifer Jones is an author, reader, handcrafter, and accidental coffee snob. She resides with her husband and pooch in wild, wonderful West Virginia. Her works have been published in various compilations from Fray'd Tag Publishing, Baer Books Press, Swyers Publishing, Haunted Waters Press, River Ram Press, Edify Fiction, and Vine Leaves Press.

Author of

~as Jennifer Howard

*The Healing Heart*
*The Steps to Karma*
*The Fume of Sighs*

~as Jennifer Jones

*La Folie Forty*
*Prompted*
*Two Strangers and a Train*

And be on the lookout for the
genre-bending short story
and poetry compilation,
*Ghosts,*
coming soon!